"Allie?" The whisper came over the phone line, oddly breathless, but so familiar and reassuring.

It had been seventeen months since she'd heard his voice, but it was just as she remembered. Strong. Solid. Relief fluttered through her chest, lifting the suffocating fear that had weighed her down for two days.

She tried to speak, but her throat closed up. Finally she managed to say, "M-Mitch?"

"Allie, where are you?"

"Oh, Mitch. I tried to call. I didn't want to leave a message on your machine. I need help."

"God, Allie. What's wrong?"

She took a deep breath. "They found me."

Dear Harlequin Intrigue Reader,

Our romantic suspense lineup this month promises to give you a lot to look forward to this holiday season!

We start off with *Full Exposure*, the second book in Debra Webb's miniseries COLBY AGENCY: INTERNAL AFFAIRS. The ongoing investigation into the agency's security leak heats up as a beautiful single mom becomes a pawn in a ruthless decimation plot. Next up…will wedding bells lead to murder? Find out in *Hijacked Honeymoon*— the fourth book in Susan Kearney's HEROES, INC. series. Then Mallory Kane continues her ULTIMATE AGENTS stories with *A Protected Witness*—an edgy mystery about a vulnerable widow who puts her life in an FBI special agent's hands.

November's ECLIPSE selection is guaranteed to tantalize you to the core! *The Man from Falcon Ridge* is a spellbinding gothic tale about a primitive falcon trainer who swoops to the rescue of a tormented woman. Does she hold the key to a grisly unsolved murder—and his heart? And you'll want to curl up in front of the fire to savor *Christmas Stalking* by Jo Leigh, which pits a sexy Santa-in-disguise against a strong-willed senator's daughter when he takes her into his protective custody. Finally this month, unwrap *Santa Assignment*, an intense mystery by Delores Fossen. The clock is ticking when a desperate father moves heaven and earth to save the woman who could give his toddler son a Christmas miracle.

Enjoy all six!

Sincerely,

Denise O'Sullivan
Senior Editor
Harlequin Intrigue

A PROTECTED WITNESS

MALLORY KANE

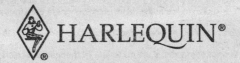

HARLEQUIN®

TORONTO • NEW YORK • LONDON
AMSTERDAM • PARIS • SYDNEY • HAMBURG
STOCKHOLM • ATHENS • TOKYO • MILAN • MADRID
PRAGUE • WARSAW • BUDAPEST • AUCKLAND

ISBN 0-373-22809-0

A PROTECTED WITNESS

Copyright © 2004 by Ricky R. Mallory

This edition published by arrangement with Harlequin Books S.A.

® and TM are trademarks of the publisher. Trademarks indicated with
® are registered in the United States Patent and Trademark Office, the
Canadian Trade Marks Office and in other countries.

www.eHarlequin.com

Printed in U.S.A.

ABOUT THE AUTHOR

Mallory Kane took early retirement from her position as assistant chief of pharmacy at a large metropolitan medical center to pursue her other loves, writing and art. She has published and won awards for science fiction and fantasy as well as romance. Mallory credits her love of books to her mother, who taught her that books are a precious resource and should be treated with loving respect. Her grandfather and her father were both steeped in the Southern tradition of oral history, and could hold an audience spellbound with their storytelling skills. Mallory aspires to be as good a storyteller as her father. She loves romantic suspense with dangerous heroes and dauntless heroines. She is also fascinated by story ideas that explore the infinite capacity of the brain to adapt and develop higher skills.

Mallory lives in Mississippi with her husband and their cat. She would be delighted to hear from readers. You can write to her c/o Harlequin Books, 233 Broadway, Suite 1001, New York, NY 10279.

Books by Mallory Kane

HARLEQUIN INTRIGUE
620—THE LAWMAN WHO LOVED HER
698—HEIR TO SECRET MEMORIES
738—BODYGUARD/HUSBAND*
789—BULLETPROOF BILLIONAIRE
809—A PROTECTED WITNESS*
*Ultimate Agents

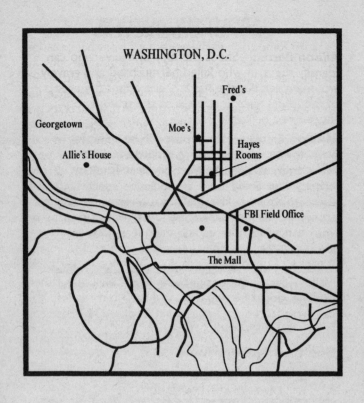

CAST OF CHARACTERS

Allison Barnes—She is the only one alive who can identify the man who killed her husband and gravely wounded her, but she has amnesia about the events of that awful night. Is it because the truth is too shocking to believe?

Mitchell Decker—He got the job he'd always wanted when his mentor was murdered. But he'd gladly give it all up, even his life, if it meant keeping Allie alive.

Joe Barnes—This FBI special agent had known too much. His execution-style murder puts his young wife's life in danger and starts a chain of events that could destroy many lives.

Frank Conover—Ruthless and ambitious, Conover likes he power of his position as a deputy assistant director of the FBI...perhaps too much.

Carmine Bongiovi—A major drug kingpin in the D.C. area, Bongiovi will stop at nothing to attain his goals, not even murder. Whose pocket is he in, and how far-reaching is his power?

Grant Irby—When he is appointed special prosecutor to investigate Joe Barnes's death, he sees an opportunity to realize his dream of being an FBI agent. All he needs is a chance and a vacant special agent position.

Hal Withers—He's a cop working undercover with Bongiovi. He has information, but is he for sale to the highest bidder?

To Michael, my own personal hero

Prologue

The man in the black topcoat rang the doorbell of the Georgetown home and smoothed his fingers over his fine leather driving gloves. The breath mint dissolving on his tongue sent a chill sharpness through his senses as he waited.

The gun in his pocket ruined the balanced custom fit of his topcoat, but that couldn't be helped. He needed the weapon instantly available, and he wasn't planning to stay long enough to take off his coat and hat. Pulling his hat farther down over his brow, he lowered his chin into the warmth of his black cashmere scarf.

This wouldn't take long.

Allison Barnes opened the door. He was surprised. Wednesday was her usual meeting with the FBI's Community Outreach Program staff. His brain raced to revise his timeline by a couple of extra seconds.

Joe Barnes's wife was over a decade younger than Joe, and striking, with high cheekbones and dark red hair. She wore a casually elegant robe and held a wineglass in her hand. For an instant she stared at him, until he lifted his chin from the scarf. He saw belated recognition dawn in her eyes.

"Hello, Allie. Is Joe home?"

"Yes. Yes, he is. Come in." She was surprised to see him, but gracious. With her sharp green gaze and her elegant assurance, she was certainly her father's daughter. It was a shame. She was lovely.

As he stepped around her, Joe appeared at the other end of the hall, looking less tense than he had in a long while. He walked straight up to him and shook his hand without removing his gloves.

"Hello, Joe." He felt another faint stab of regret. He had been valuable, in his way. Still, it couldn't be helped. "Surprised to see me?"

The special agent in charge of the FBI's Division of Unsolved Mysteries looked at his visitor with a mixture of resolve and fear in his eyes. He knew exactly why he'd come.

"I'm not changing my mind," he said, lifting his chin and casting a worried glance toward his wife. "Can't we talk about this tomorrow?"

"This will just take a minute." The man reached into his pocket and closed his hand around his gun. Behind him, Allison started toward them, her shoes clicking on the Italian tiles.

"May I take your hat and coat—" she started as he lifted the gun from his pocket and shot Joe between the eyes.

His wife screamed.

He turned to put a bullet into her temple as she pushed past him, but she fooled him. She didn't rush toward her fallen husband. Instead, he barely caught a glimpse of her ashen face as she whirled and ran in the opposite direction. In front of her on the hall table was a telephone. She reached for it. Cursing, he pulled the trigger. Twice.

Her body arched as the bullets slammed into her slender back. She fell to her knees, then crumpled forward on the tile floor, her dark red hair floating down like a dropped silken scarf.

He started toward her, his gun aimed at the back of her head. The piercing sound of a siren split the silence of the night, and somewhere close, dogs barked.

The man in the black topcoat couldn't afford to stop even for an instant. He knew exactly how much time had passed. Impeccable timing and flawless planning had gotten him where he was today. Allison's unexpected presence had cost him three seconds. He had to leave now.

Stepping around her body to avoid the fast-spreading pool of blood, he walked out the door. He pulled his hat down, tucking his chin into his scarf. He slipped into the sleek dark car and drove away.

Chapter One

Seventeen months later, early summer

"Angela? Weren't you going to leave early today?"

Allison Barnes looked up from her computer screen and smiled at her boss, Dr. Timothy White, head of the Criminal Justice Department at Colorado State University. It had been seventeen months since the murder of her husband of eight years, but she still wasn't comfortable with her new name, Angela Martin, or her new life. Or the lack of progress in the investigation. The information from her Witness Security Program contact was frustratingly sparse. But she knew how methodically the FBI worked. And how closely they guarded their information. She'd had plenty of experience.

Until she regained her memory of the events of that night, or until the FBI got a major break in the case, she would probably hear nothing beyond the short monthly update from her WSP contact.

"Angela?"

She realized she hadn't answered her boss. "I'm almost done with your slide presentation, Dr. White," she said. "Then I'm out of here. I've got popcorn and car-

toons for the kids tonight and ice cream afterward."
Once a month, she spent an evening entertaining a
group of grade-school children whose lives had been
touched by the actions of drunken drivers. It was a
cause dear to her heart. She'd been ten when her mother
was killed by a drunk driver, leaving her and her father,
FBI Deputy Assistant Director for Criminal Investigations Harry MacNeal, alone.

She had started her first program for children in D.C.,
where it had been very successful. Being able to do the
same thing here in Grand Junction had gone a long way
toward keeping her sane during the months of isolation
and secrecy.

Her boss gave her the boyish smile that made him so
popular with the female students on campus. "Sounds
like fun. One of these nights, you'll have to let me tag
along. I love cartoons and ice cream."

She turned back to the computer screen, the familiar
guilt washing over her. It was so hard to act normal when
her entire life was built on a lie. She didn't like deceiv-
ing people, especially someone as nice as Tim White.

She glanced toward his office door. Maybe he was
the reason she'd been so preoccupied lately. He'd made
no secret of the fact that he wanted to date her. Was she
beginning to long for a normal life? One where she
could go out, have fun and be herself?

She almost laughed. She could never be herself
again. Allison MacNeal Barnes no longer existed.

As she worked on the presentation, part of her mind
dwelled on the night that had changed her life forever.
She didn't remember anything about the shooting or
about Mitch Decker, her husband's friend and protégé,
arriving at their house in time to save her life.

All she remembered was the dimly lit intensive care unit, and floating in and out of consciousness while the heart monitor beeped rhythmically and the dull pain thudded mercilessly inside her.

Each time she'd woken up, Mitch had been there beside her, his low gentle voice echoing in her head.

Allie, be brave.

Allie, I'm so sorry about Joe.

Allie, don't cry.

Mitch Decker, another nice guy, but Mitch was nice in a darker, more dangerous way. He was no mild-mannered professor who would like children and ice cream. He was an FBI agent, like her husband. Like her father.

Mitch had lost his friend and mentor that night, but he hadn't left her side. He'd sat beside her hospital bed, his lean powerful body a bulwark against the men in dark suits who guarded her door. His honest blue eyes were dark with grief and compassion, and his hand steady as it cradled hers.

Tears clogged her throat. How many nights since then had she lain awake, longing for his steady strong hand, longing for someone who knew her and who understood her loss, her confusion and fear?

Had Mitch endured hours of intense questioning, too? Had he been able to tell Special Prosecutor Grant Irby any more than she had about her husband's supposed dealings with the criminal underworld of D.C.? Mitch had known Joe. He'd have told them the same thing she had—there was no way Joe Barnes had been involved in anything crooked. Her husband had been a decent man.

She glanced at her watch and forced her attention back to the slide presentation. She had to concentrate.

Ten minutes later, with her jacket and purse in hand, she hurried into Dr. White's office to drop off the disk containing the presentation.

"Thanks for letting me leave early."

"No problem. Have fun tonight. My flight leaves at 7:00 a.m. tomorrow, so I won't see you until Monday. Maybe by then, you'll change your mind and go out to dinner with me." He lifted his eyebrows and smiled hopefully.

Allison considered her boss. He was handsome and charming, only a few years older than her, and his career was as far from the FBI as she could ever hope for.

Ever since that night eight years ago, when she'd found her father lying in his driveway, dead from a single bullet to the back of his head, she'd wished for just this kind of quiet, uneventful life. It was ironic that now, because her life was in danger, she'd gotten her wish.

So why was she resisting Tim's gentle overtures? There was a very good chance that even if the FBI solved Joe's murder, she'd spend the rest of her life in Grand Junction as Angela Martin. After all, there was nothing to go back to in D.C. The murderer and the FBI had seen to that.

Nothing to go back to. Her heart ached at the sadness of those words. Her father and her husband were dead. She was alone. Feeling as if she were betraying Joe's memory and acutely conscious that every word she breathed was a lie, she gave Dr. White a little smile and relented. "I'd love to have dinner with you."

LATE THAT EVENING, Allison drove to her apartment, still smiling over how much fun the children had had.

She felt surprisingly content and relaxed. Taking the step of accepting a date as Angela Martin had been a good idea. She was actually looking forward to next week.

But right now, she was pleasantly tired and ready to go to sleep. Yawning as she turned the key in the dead bolt on her apartment door, it took a second for her to notice that there was no resistance. The door was unlocked.

The shock of adrenaline hit her like ice water. She froze, expecting the door to jerk open and reveal the faceless monster who had destroyed her life. She forced her trembling legs to back away.

As she hurried down the stairs to the manager's apartment, she pulled out her cell phone to dial the preset number of her Witness Security Program contact, even though she knew all she would hear were three rings and then the beep of an answering machine. She could leave a message and soon her contact would call her back.

She heard a click. But only one ring sounded before a shrill tone made her jump. Frowning, she looked at the display. She had dialed the correct number, but it didn't sound the same.

She turned off the phone, her heart pounding faster and faster.

She knocked on the apartment manager's door, the few seconds until it opened stretching her nerves taut as a rubber band.

"Mr. Ray, were you in my apartment today?"

The balding man in his mid-fifties squinted at her through the blue thread of smoke drifting up from the cigarette dangling from his lips. "Nope."

"My door is unlocked. Did you see anyone?" Her voice quavered.

"You prob'ly forgot—" He met her gaze and stopped. He sighed deeply. "I'll go check it out." A long frail ash quivered on the end of the cigarette as he stepped outside. "Like I've got time…."

"Maybe you should call the police," Allison said as she followed him.

"Is the lock broke?"

"No, it's just unlocked. I didn't go inside."

The man stopped her at the bottom of the steps. "Stay here then. I'll go check, make sure there's no *burglars* in there." He chuckled at his own joke.

"Mr. Ray, please call the police."

He dismissed her with a shake of his head and lumbered up the stairs to her door. Allison put one foot on the stairs, debating about following him. What if she had forgotten to lock the door? What if her phone had sounded funny because the battery was low?

No. The two things weren't coincidence. Something was wrong.

"Mr. Ray—wait!" she called, but he'd already disappeared inside her apartment.

Allison expected him to appear again immediately, bellyaching about bothering him for nothing, but he didn't. She took an instinctive step backward. Had she just sent Mr. Ray into danger?

Suddenly a deafening roar filled her ears, red and yellow flames flashed before her and black smoke belched out through the open door of her apartment.

Before her brain even registered the heat of the explosion, she found herself on her rear at the foot of the stairs, the healed wounds in her back protesting painfully.

Allison screamed. Hot air stung her eyes and nose. Her skin felt tight. She couldn't breathe. She tried to pick herself up off the ground, but couldn't keep her balance.

Her cell phone lay a few feet away where she'd dropped it. She scrambled for it, scratching her palms and knees on the hardwood floor, and dialed 911, quickly reporting the explosion and the address. Then she crawled back over to the stair rail. She gripped it.

Hot.

Fiery reds and oranges flickered across her vision like a swirling burning kaleidoscope. Trembling, she used the heated railing to steady herself. She tried to climb the stairs, but the roar and flames continued and the force of the heat pushed her back.

Sirens wailed, growing louder. People erupted from nearby apartments, shouting and screaming.

"He's in there!" she cried. "Mr. Ray is in there!"

A couple of burly guys ran up the stairs, but couldn't get close to the door because of the heat.

The entrance doors crashed open as firemen burst in. The sirens' screams echoed through the halls as police cars screeched to a halt.

"Anyone inside?" a fireman yelled as they started unrolling hose.

"The super," one of the men called out.

Allison started to step forward, to tell the fireman what had happened.

"Whose apartment is this?" a policeman shouted from behind her. "Who knows something about this?"

Allison stopped.

Whose apartment...

It was her apartment, and she couldn't say a word.

She couldn't stick around long enough to find out if Mr. Ray was alive or dead. She had to get away. Her apartment had been blown up.

They'd found her.

"YOU WANT TO tell me how you Einsteins managed to blow up the apartment manager?" Carmine Bongiovi jerked the expensive Cuban cigar out of his mouth and brushed a speck of fallen ash off the top of his polished desk, careful not to leave a fingerprint. "Never mind. It don't matter now."

The man on the other end of the phone started a litany of explanations about how they couldn't help who'd gone into the target's apartment first.

"Shut up. What about her?"

"Headed back to D.C., we think."

"You think." Bongiovi started to shove the cigar back into his mouth, looked at it and then set it carefully on the edge of a lead crystal dish. He hated to waste a good Cuban by smoking it when he was frustrated. "You better be sure."

"We followed her to Interstate 70. Don't worry. We'll pick up her trail."

Bongiovi toyed with the Fabergé egg his wife had given him and nodded to himself. It had taken seventeen months to locate Allison Barnes. He'd known from the start that the official word about her death wasn't true. She'd been placed in the Witness Security Program until she regained her lost memories of the night she was shot.

Knowing she'd been involved with the FBI's Community Outreach Program in D.C. which worked with children affected by drunk driving, Bongiovi had put out feelers all over the United States for similar organizations. Sure enough, a woman fitting her description had shown up on the radar in Grand Junction, Colorado.

"Make sure you do. I ain't planning on losing her now!"

Bongiovi had done many jobs such as this over the years. Back in the day, he'd taken care of them personally. Take his first big job. Killing Deputy Assistant Director Harry MacNeal had been a huge risk for the small-time thug he'd been back then.

But his risk had paid off. Now, eight years later, he was the undisputed kingpin of the D.C. underworld. Bongiovi frowned and picked up his cigar, then put it down again.

It was ironic that the job that had cemented his position and this recent one both involved Allison Barnes, MacNeal's daughter.

An even bigger irony was the growing yearning inside him to leave this life behind. To realize the dream that had been born the day he'd held his first child in his arms. These days, the city's most ruthless crime boss found more satisfaction in watching his little girls play with dolls. He longed for the simple, safe life he'd known as a boy working in his father's deli.

He sighed and dialed another number. "Yeah. A little glitch in our plans. Mrs. Barnes is still alive." He listened. "She's on her way back here. Don't worry. I'm on top of it."

The voice on the other end of the phone spoke.

Bongiovi rolled his eyes. "Right. I understand your terms perfectly." *Arrogant bastard.* Bongiovi compressed his lips as he listened. "All's I need from you is one thing. Where's she going?"

He listened.

"Yeah. Makes sense. He never left her side in the hospital." He tossed the Fabergé egg into the air and caught it, then carefully set the gold enamel egg, with its inlaid precious and semiprecious stones, down on its stand and hung up the phone.

Outside his office door, he heard the low, melodic voice of his wife and the excited chatter of his older daughter.

He smiled to himself. The seventeen months he'd spent searching for Joe Barnes's widow had not been wasted.

He'd find her. It would only be a matter of time.

A new plan began to form. He ran his fingertips along the crease in his custom-tailored slacks and picked up his cigar, flicking the lighter and puffing away.

SPECIAL COUNSEL Grant Irby hung up his phone and dug in his pocket for a handkerchief. He carefully blotted sweat off his upper lip and neck. The news from the U.S. Marshal's office was not what he'd expected, nor was it what he'd feared.

Allison Barnes was missing. She'd survived an explosion at her apartment, but before she could be questioned by the police and the fire department, she had disappeared.

Irby had been investigating the murder of Joe Barnes for seventeen months. But the investigation was progressing like a tortoise with a full belly.

"As special counsel on the Joe Barnes murder case, we wanted to notify you first thing," the deputy U.S. Marshal had told him. "Of course, we've already notified Deputy Assistant Director Conover."

Irby had thanked him and disconnected. He pushed his two hundred and seventy pounds out of the tight confines of his office chair and stepped over to the air vent, letting the cool air flow over his hot face.

Of course, they'd notified DAD Conover first. He'd been Joe's boss at the Bureau. Irby was just a GS-13 lawyer assigned to the FBI. The impossible task of digging out the facts behind Special Agent Barnes's execution-style murder and the near fatal shooting of his wife had fallen to him.

Anger too hot for the air vent to cool flushed his face. If things had gone the way they should have years ago, he'd be the FBI agent, and some other barely competent lawyer would be reporting to *him*.

Grant Irby, Special Agent in Charge. There was nothing he wouldn't do to have that sign on his desk.

You were qualified and referred for consideration, but someone else was chosen.

Qualified—he'd seen that word three times now. Just not qualified enough. The first time he'd applied, Mitchell Decker had been hired. Then, after Harry MacNeal's death, when Frank Conover moved into the deputy assistant director's position and Joe Barnes took over the Division of Unsolved Mysteries, Irby had applied again and been turned down again.

Then, after Barnes's death, when Decker had been promoted, he'd applied a third time. Another wave of anger heated his face. It wasn't fair. He would make an exceptional agent.

If he solved Joe Barnes's murder, things would be different. Conover would notice him, recognize his potential and finally give him the job he'd always wanted—FBI special agent. An excitement that was almost sexual buzzed through him as his fingers itched to hold the coveted badge, to fire a gun in the performance of his duties.

So Allison Barnes had miraculously survived a deadly explosion and was on the run. Irby had as good a chance as anyone of finding her, now that she was out from under the protection of the WSP.

Irby looked at his watch. He had seven minutes until the scheduled conference call that would take up the rest of his afternoon. He dabbed his burning cheeks one last time and sat down to compose himself. Before he even caught his breath, his intercom buzzed. Irby glared at it. The conference call was early. Why couldn't people structure their time like he did?

Sighing, he punched the button with his trigger finger.

IT WAS AFTER two o'clock in the morning when Mitchell Decker unlocked the door of his apartment overlooking Woodley Park. He'd stopped by the office first. As he'd expected, Eric was still there. Eric Baldwyn, profiler for the Division of Unsolved Mysteries, was working with the Montgomery County Police Department on a series of rapes and attempted rapes that appeared to be connected. When Eric was in the middle of a profile, he didn't eat or sleep. Often, he didn't even talk.

Mitch had given him the usual lecture about taking care of himself, and Eric had given Mitch his usual promise that he'd do better.

Then Mitch had looked in on the other member of his staff who was burning the midnight oil. Natasha Rudolph. The division's computer wizard was asleep at her keyboard, her blond head propped against one fist. Her signature black turtleneck and slacks blended into the shadows cast by the pale light of her computer monitor. He tried to exit without waking her, but he'd never seen anyone who could come within forty feet of the young Russian immigrant without her knowing it.

"Morning, Mitch," she said, sitting up and stretching. "Welcome back. I found our guy."

"The Davidson kidnapping? Is it the father?"

"Yep. Rumors of his untimely death three years ago were greatly exaggerated."

Decker had nodded in satisfaction. "You called Storm?"

She nodded. "I left a message. You know he's in bed. Maybe asleep, maybe not," she said wryly. "I'm waiting to hear back so I can fax him the intel." She squinted at him. "How about you? How are you doing?"

Mitch had smiled tiredly and assured Natasha that he was fine.

He was. And glad to be home. He nudged his front door closed and dropped his bags on the floor of the foyer. He considered D.C. his home. His first and only home.

His childhood had been a constant series of apartments and hotel rooms as his father swooped in on companies in trouble, did his thing and then moved on.

Mitch grabbed a bottle of water from his refrigerator, thinking about the past week and his father's unexpected death.

His sister Elizabeth had taken care of the arrangements before Mitch had even arrived in San Francisco. All he'd had to do was be there. Liz was just like their father, driven, ruthless, obsessed. So naturally, every last detail about the funeral was flawless.

Mitch had had nothing to do, which had given him plenty of time to reflect on why, although he and his father had been estranged for years, the old man's death left such a big hole inside him. A hole almost as big as the one left by the death of his boss and mentor, Joe Barnes. He hadn't come up with a good answer.

He'd never admired their father the way Liz had. To Mitch, John Decker was an emotional wasteland and an entrepreneurial piranha. He attacked failing companies using ruthless tactics and his legendary instinct.

As Mitch finished the water, his eye was caught by the message light on his telephone. He was surprised to see it blinking. He didn't get many messages on his home phone, and he'd checked them from San Francisco a day or so ago.

He pressed Play and jotted down the originating number of the first message.

There was nothing there. A fraction of a second of silence, then a hang-up. Mitch looked back at the number. He didn't recognize the area code.

He played the message again, concentrating on the silence. Could he hear anything? Nope. Just dead air, then the sound of the receiver being cradled. So it wasn't a cell phone. Nor had he heard the familiar click of a computer switch that signaled a cold call from a telemarketer.

He went on to the second message, writing down another unfamiliar number. This time, the caller stayed on the line a heartbeat longer, but Mitch still couldn't distinguish any sounds. He thought he'd heard a car horn and maybe the echo of traffic whizzing past. Was the caller in a phone booth?

He pulled out his cell phone and punched speed dial.

"Nat, good. You're still there. Run a couple of phone numbers for me."

He gave her the numbers and waited. After a few seconds, Natasha made a satisfied sound.

"Here we go. The first one is a phone booth outside of Grand Junction, Colorado. The second…" She paused and he heard the keyboard clicking. "The second came from a phone booth in St. Louis, Missouri. Everything okay?"

"Fine," he said distractedly. Two phone booths in two different states, twenty hours apart. "Thanks, Nat."

"Anytime, boss."

"Now go home. Don't show up again until Monday."

"I'm still trying to trace that hacker—"

"That's not a top priority. Go."

"Yes, *Dad!*" She made fun of his fatherly concern for his staff, but Mitch knew she appreciated it. She had no family that he was aware of.

He pulled up an atlas program on his computer and traced a line between the two towns Natasha had mentioned. They were both along I-70. He queried the quickest route between Grand Junction, Colorado, and D.C. The blue line traced I-70 through St. Louis and all the way through Pennsylvania to where it joined I-270 toward D.C. And it confirmed what he was thinking. Whoever had called him was headed this way.

He touched the little circle on the computer screen that represented Grand Junction with his fingertip, trying to dismiss the first thought that popped into his head. But it wouldn't stay dismissed.

He took a deep breath, imagining the subtle scent of lavender. Shaking his head, he tried unsuccessfully to stop the vision of dark red hair and deep sea foam-green eyes that not even seventeen months' distance had banished.

The calls were wrong numbers, he told himself. But that wasn't likely. Two wrong numbers, twenty hours apart, on a direct route to D.C.? It was too much of a coincidence. Mitch didn't believe in coincidences.

But the only thing that made sense was preposterous, wasn't it?

He knew that protected witnesses were usually relocated to landlocked states. Since most of them were criminals themselves, it served the U.S. Marshal's Service to keep them in places that didn't offer a quick escape route to a border.

"Damn, Allie. Is it you?" His whole body tensed with worry, his heart clenching in his chest. All this time, and not a day had passed that she hadn't been on his mind.

Was she in trouble? Every instinct told him it was her, but he didn't like to depend on instinct. He never had. Instinct was like his father. Unreliable.

For one frightening moment—after she'd been whisked away in the middle of the night and her obituary had appeared in *The Washington Post,* Mitch had felt as if she had actually died.

Rationally, he'd known she'd been put in the Witness Security Program for her safety until she regained her lost memories of that night. But he'd been there—he'd seen her lying on the floor in a dark and spreading pool of her own blood and watched as she was rolled into the operating room with a ventilator breathing for her and a thoracic specialist shouting at the nurses to hurry.

She was safe now. Safe and far away from D.C. There was no logical reason for her to call him.

Unless she was in trouble, he argued with himself. But that wasn't logical, either. He wasn't authorized to help her.

If she needed help, she'd do what she'd been instructed to do—call her Witness Security Program contact. The U.S. Marshal's Service would immediately move her to a safe place and give her another new identity.

And Mitch still wouldn't know where she was.

He showered and climbed into bed, but when he closed his eyes, all he saw was Allie's pale, lovely face against the brilliant white of the intensive care unit sheets. All he heard was the pinging of the heart monitor that measured out her life beat by beat.

He tossed back the covers and got up, brushing his hand over his short damp hair. There was no way in hell he was going to get any sleep tonight.

Standing at the window overlooking the park, he let the memories and guilt wash over him like a summer storm—unwelcome and uncomfortable, but unavoidable. Joe Barnes had been more of a father to Mitch than his own father ever had. Joe had been a true friend and mentor.

He'd trusted his instincts that awful night, and the results had been tragic. If he'd gotten to their home just a few minutes sooner, maybe Joe wouldn't be dead, and Allie wouldn't have been sent away.

He wondered if she was happy, making a new life for herself, getting past the tragedy. Maybe she'd met someone new.

Mitch swore and wiped his face, rubbing his palm across the stubble that roughened his chin.

Abruptly he turned away from the window and the

feelings he had never—and now would never—let himself explore, because Allie had been his boss's wife. His gaze settled on the phone and her face rose again in his mind in haunting detail.

Mitch frowned, fighting to banish the vision. But the instinct he tried to temper with logic reared, sharpening the classically beautiful lines of her face in his memory. Her green eyes pleaded with him. That little worried frown marred her forehead.

If it was Allie and she was reaching out from behind the fortress of the Witness Security Program to contact him, then something horrible had happened. Something that made her feel the WSP couldn't protect her.

The skin of his scalp tightened and his shoulders cramped with tension.

Allie's life was in danger.

THE PHONE HADN'T RUNG during the night. But Mitch still hadn't slept. He'd lain in the dark, heart pounding, thoughts racing. Why hadn't she called again? Where was she? Had something happened to her?

He tried to work the next day, but his mind wasn't on his job. By the end of the day, he'd only made it through the top four items in the stack his superefficient secretary had collected for him while he was in San Francisco.

The day was typical, punctuated by phone calls, discussions with various members of his staff, a luncheon with the special agents in charge of the other divisions under Deputy Assistant Director Frank Conover, and paperwork.

Mitch stopped halfway through a stack of forms that needed his signature, laid down his pen and flexed his cramped fingers. One of the most frustrating parts of any government job was the paperwork. Today, it was torturous. He couldn't sit here any longer. He wanted to go home, to be there when Allie called again.

If it was her, his logical brain reminded him. He glanced at the clock, a little surprised to see how late it was. After seven. He was alone in the suite. He stood and arched his neck.

As he shrugged into his jacket, his desk phone rang.

He reached for it, his heart leaping in his chest. It might be Allie.

ALLIE TRIED TO ignore the mixture of disgusting smells that swirled around the inside of the glass phone booth as she listened to the ringing. She'd heard that ring many times. It was the office number of the special agent in charge of the Division of Unsolved Mysteries. Joe's number. Now Mitch Decker's.

When she'd jumped into her car forty-eight hours ago, she hadn't known what she was going to do. She'd just known she couldn't stay in Grand Junction and answer questions about why her apartment had been blown up.

She'd tried to call her WSP contact again, but her cell phone still sounded strange. Had the people who wanted her dead somehow tampered with her phone, or with her contact number?

She'd turned off the government issue phone and headed east, toward the only person she knew she could trust—Mitch Decker.

It was ironic that he worked for the same organization that had destroyed her life. She'd never wanted to be associated with the FBI again. The one good thing about the Witness Security Program was that it had separated her from the agency that had caused her father's death, her husband's death and very nearly her own.

So why, at the first sign of trouble, had she run toward them? She knew the answer. She hadn't run toward the FBI. She was running to Mitch.

Mitch was an honorable man, and he'd been a good friend to both Joe and her. The night before the shooting, the three of them had met for dinner at her favorite restaurant, as they did every few weeks or so. When Joe had received a call and had to leave, Mitch had seen Allie home and waited with her for hours, until it became obvious that Joe wasn't going to show up.

Then after the shooting, he'd been there beside her in the hospital every time she'd opened her eyes, until they'd taken her away. His soothing voice had eased her pain. His presence had made her feel safe.

And right now, she prayed that the last thing he'd said to her was the truth.

If you ever need me, I'll be here, Allie. I promise.

The phone rang again. He was probably gone for the day. Panic sheared her breath.

She glanced around the deserted parking lot, debating whether to try his home phone again or just get back in her car and keep driving.

Her limbs felt paralyzed with terror. If she couldn't find Mitch, she had nowhere else to go.

"Decker."

She jumped. His dark sure voice echoed through the phone line like the reverberation of a big deep bell.

Her hand tightened around the dirty pay phone receiver. Her pulse pounded in her temple. She hadn't realized how afraid she'd been that she wouldn't find him. She sighed in relief.

"Allie?" The whisper came over the phone line, no longer bell-like, oddly breathless, but so familiar, so reassuring.

It had been seventeen months since she'd heard his voice, but it was just as she remembered. Strong. Solid. Relief fluttered through her chest, lifting the suffocating fear that had weighed her down for two days.

She tried to speak, but her throat closed up. Finally, she managed to say, "M-Mitch?"

"Allie, where are you?"

"Oh, Mitch. I tried to call. I didn't want to leave a message on your machine. I need help."

"God, Allie. What's wrong?"

She took a deep breath. "They found me."

Chapter Two

Allie could hear Mitch's sharp intake of breath through the phone line. "Who found you? Are you all right? Allie, are you here in D.C.?"

She felt perilously close to tears. It was so good to hear his voice. He could help her. He'd know what to do.

"I've been driving for two days. I'm in a phone booth—" She paused. She'd seen the phone booth from the interstate, in the poorly lit parking lot of a gas station, so she'd exited.

What road *was* she on?

"Where? What are the cross streets?"

She squinted at a street sign. "I think it's Seventh Street. Seventh and Decatur. A gas station parking lot."

"That's in a really rough section."

"I had to find a phone booth. I can't use my cell phone. They've tampered with it."

"Okay," Mitch said quickly. "We'll talk when I get there. You're about fifteen minutes away, if I can avoid the traffic. Is the gas station open?"

Allie looked at the tiny building and the sleepy-eyed employee behind the counter. "Yes. There's a convenience store."

"Go inside and wait with the clerk. I'm on my way."

"Okay. Mitch?" She clenched her teeth in an effort to stop her voice from quavering. Now that she'd found him, the tension that had knotted her muscles relaxed, and she trembled.

"Thanks," she said, but she was talking to a dead phone. He had hung up. Typically, he was wasting no time. He had the information he needed and he was acting on it. His brisk instructions and immediate unquestioning response were familiar and comforting.

As Allie hung up the phone and walked across the parking lot toward the brightly lit store, she realized Mitch had called her name before she'd said a word.

He'd known it was her. A place inside her that had ached with loneliness and fear for seventeen months relaxed.

She wasn't completely alone. She had Mitch.

A MAN SITTING in a dark vehicle on a street across from the FBI field office put down his cold coffee and punched a preset number on his cell phone.

"Got her. She called the office. He's on his way. Seventh and Decatur. A convenience store."

He drained the last of his cold coffee and turned off the phone.

"Hey, Norm," he called to the driver, who was asleep behind the wheel. "Norm!"

Norm sat up.

"Let's go. We got 'em."

MITCH LOCKED UP the offices, cursing the time it took to check out through the building's intense security. He got into his car and took off, whipping through side streets and working his way toward Decatur Street.

He called the phone booth's number, but the phone's ring echoed unchecked. He sighed with relief. She'd done what he'd told her to do.

Allie had experience with the FBI, and her father and husband had given her a clear understanding of safety precautions. She'd sensed that there was something wrong with her cell phone, so she'd turned it off.

He nodded his approval. Calling from pay phones along the way had been a good idea. It had given him information while not being traceable back to her. She'd also been smart not to leave him a message. She didn't know him well enough to know he'd never play his messages if anyone were within earshot.

An SUV tried to sneak through a red light, almost sideswiping him. He veered, cursing, then straightened and continued on.

He concentrated on driving, but a part of his brain was consumed with her. Her voice—so familiar, so frightened—had made his heart ache. He'd known it was her as soon as he'd heard her soft breath. He'd never been anything but her husband's friend and employee, but if he lived for eternity, her voice would still be the most beautiful sound he'd ever hear.

Would she look the same? Had the Witness Security Program changed her appearance? He hoped not. It would be a crime to tamper with perfection.

Her beauty was imprinted on his brain like an engraving. He remembered the way she'd looked that night at the restaurant, and afterward in her kitchen as they had waited for Joe to come home. Slender and lovely, her skin was as fine and translucent as porcelain, her eyes wide and intelligent. She had hair the color of copper that moved when she talked, and a tiny frown that appeared when she was worried, as she had been that night.

But on the heels of that memory came another, the memory of her face down, her blood staining the cold tile.

The last time he'd seen her, she'd smiled bravely and squeezed his hand as they took her away to surgery. He'd promised her he'd be there for her. But he hadn't been able to keep his promise. The next morning, she was gone. The ICU personnel had given him the official line.

Allison Barnes died in surgery.

Of course she hadn't died. She'd been relocated by the Witness Security Program. But knowing that hadn't helped as the nurse's crisp voice said, *I'm sorry, sir.* His whole body had frozen for a millisecond, until the logical side of his brain reminded him that she was still alive and safe. And out of his reach.

He'd always kept a respectable distance around Joe's wife, but in that awful instant, he'd known she meant more to him than he'd ever acknowledged.

The sign for Decatur Street loomed ahead. He turned. There, near the corner of Decatur and Seventh, was the empty phone booth. He saw two figures, clearly outlined by the fluorescent lights, inside the convenience store.

His breath whooshed out in a huge sigh. She was safe.

He hadn't told her what his car looked like. He headed toward the front door, planning to pull up close so she could see him.

A flash of metal caught his eye. A dark car eased toward the door from the opposite direction.

Experience and excellent night vision told Mitch that the passenger side window of the dark car was down and the occupant, whose face was hidden by some sort of dark mask, held a hand gun trained on the glass doors of the store.

Mitch saw the tiny red dot of the laser sight, bright as fresh blood on the front of Allie's shirt.

He had no time.

He drew his service weapon from his shoulder holster and hit the gas, forcing his car between the dark car and the doorway. The bullet meant for Allie hit his passenger door. He jabbed the buttons that lowered his driver's side and passenger windows.

"Allie, get down!" he yelled as he fired through the passenger window. The bullet ricocheted off the other car's frame as the shooter ducked.

The car's engine revved.

He fired off two more rounds, putting major cracks in their windshield just to show them he was serious. Another slug hit his vehicle.

The dark car spun its tires and raced toward him. He fired again. At the last possible second, the car whipped left, scraped Mitch's fender and then screamed out of the parking lot. Mitch jumped out, his gun at the ready, and squinted at the fast disappearing license tag in the dimness of the streetlights. It was a D.C. tag obscured with dirt.

He thought he made out the first three numbers. He'd have Natasha run them.

He tried to put faces to the two figures he'd seen through the windshield, but the smoked glass, their masks, and the spiderweb of cracks caused by his shots had removed any hope of identifying them.

He surveyed the parking lot, assuring himself that no one else was around, before turning toward the store. He prayed Allie was all right.

She stepped through the glass doors, her green eyes wide and filled with fear. Mitch drank in the sight of her. She'd lost weight. Her hair was carelessly caught up in a barrette. Her face was as pale as it had been when she was in the hospital, and her movements were jerky and unsure, but her head was high.

Mitch stared, stunned by the reality of her standing in front of him. He'd thought he'd never see her again, never be able to tell her how sorry he was that he'd let her and Joe down. He wanted to touch her, to assure himself she was real and not just another dream.

"Allie, are you all right?" he croaked.

She nodded, walking toward him. He reached for her. As she stepped into the curve of his arms, he steeled himself against the feelings.

He'd never held her, never thought he would, other than to accept a quick kiss on the cheek or a handshake. To his chagrin, his arms shook with relief, his throat constricted with emotion, and his body surged with shameful, unwanted desire.

She felt small and fragile, even though at five feet eight inches, she was only five inches shorter than his six foot one. Her shoulders were stiff, a fine trembling shook her frame and the wetness of her tears against his neck seared his skin.

For an instant, he just held her, his head spinning with her agonizingly familiar scent of lavender and cinnamon. He'd never smelled anything that smelled like her.

"Thank God you're here," she whispered shakily.

Immediately, his logical side took over. The dark car may have gone for the moment, but the two of them were exposed in the empty parking lot and Allie was in danger.

He gently pushed her away enough to look at her face. Her eyes were wet and red-rimmed and she had no makeup on, but she was still the most beautiful woman he'd ever seen. Joe had been a lucky man.

Joe. Her husband. His friend.

"We've got to get out of here," he said gruffly, forcing himself not to rub his thumb along her pale cheeks to dry her tears. "I don't want to spend the whole night explaining to the local police why an FBI special agent was shooting at an unknown subject to protect a dead woman."

Allie's head jerked at his words, and he regretted being so blunt, but until he figured out how the killer had found her, he didn't have time for niceties. He wasn't taking any chances, not with her life.

She blotted her cheeks with her palms. "Of course. You're right."

His arm still around her shoulders, Mitch opened the passenger door of his car for her to climb in. Inside the glass walls of the convenience store, the clerk held a phone to his ear, talking and gesturing wildly.

He doubted the man was talking to his wife. More likely he'd dialed 911. Sure enough, as he tilted his head, the sound of faraway sirens reached his ears.

"That your car or a rental?" He nodded toward a white Chrysler with Colorado plates.

"It's mine."

He got a small, high-intensity flashlight out of his

glove box. "Stay here and honk the horn if you see the police or that black car coming back."

Mitch shone the flashlight all around the Chrysler, looking for a tracking device, a GPS receiver, anything that would explain how someone had managed to find her in a gas station on an unremarkable road just off the interstate in Washington, D.C.

After a brisk and concentrated search of the most logical places and a few not-so-logical ones, Mitch had to make a decision. If there was a tracking device in her car, it was well hidden.

He assessed the vehicle for a full five seconds, conscious of the sirens drawing closer. He knew a couple of gunshots in a neighborhood like this didn't send up the kind of alarms it might in, say, Georgetown. Around here, sirens wailed all through the night.

Still, he had to assume the sirens were heading their way. There was no time to get rid of the car or hide the identity of its owner. It wouldn't take the local police long to trace it back to Grand Junction, Colorado, and whatever name the Witness Security Program had set up for Allie. It would take them longer to figure out that the person who owned the car wasn't real. The WSP was good at creating false identities.

That would give Mitch time to notify them of her whereabouts and get her back into safe hiding. It would give him a good start on figuring out how the killer had found her.

He jumped into his car and started the engine.

"Was there something in my car?"

Mitch put the car in gear. "Not that I found. How did they know you were here?"

"I don't know."

"What about your cell phone?"

"It's been turned off since I left Grand Junction. I tried twice to call my contact, but both times I got a peculiar sound."

"Isn't your contact number just an answering machine?"

"Yes, but there was a click, and it only rang once instead of three times, and the tone was different. Shrill."

Mitch nodded. She'd done the right thing. "You called them from a pay phone though, right?"

"Yes. All I could do was leave a message that I would contact them when I was in a safe place. Then I called you. I didn't know where else to go. Joe trusted you. So do I."

Her words pierced his heart like a .38 slug. Joe had trusted him. He had an obligation to keep Joe's widow safe.

He drove carefully, not wanting to attract any more attention than he had to. If the convenience store attendant had written down his car tag, he was going to have a lot to explain. He didn't want to have to start the explanations before he'd talked to Allie.

He got on the interstate, heading on into the city.

"Where are we going?" she asked.

"A hotel. The locals will be on me soon enough if the clerk saw my car tag. And even if he didn't, I need to buy some time. I want some answers."

ALLIE SAT IN one of the plush chairs in the hotel room, wrapped in an oversize white terry-cloth robe with the hotel's logo on it, her feet shoved into their complimentary slippers. The hot shower had made her feel better, but her limbs were still shaky, and now her eyes were red and swollen. Standing under the hot spray, she'd cried. She hadn't intended to. But with the steam cocooning her, and knowing she was safe with Mitch in the next room, she'd surprised herself by breaking down.

She hated to cry. From the time her mother had died, her father had drilled into her that tears were a sign of weakness. Self-indulgence led to mistakes, and mistakes could be fatal. She'd tried so hard to be strong, to keep her wits about her, and she'd made it this far. She'd found Mitch.

So for the first time in seventeen months, she'd let go. The brief release had driven some of the tension from her body.

But that was it. No more crying. No more self-pity. There was no time. Someone was trying to kill her.

Mitch came out of the dressing area. When his gaze met hers, his usually solemn face creased in a quick smile.

She remembered his smile. It was surprising and welcome, like a sudden glimpse of the sun on a gloomy day.

"I made some coffee," he said, sitting down on the end of the bed and propping his elbows on his knees. "It'll be ready in a minute." His tone was gentle, reassuring. The sound of it conjured memories of the dim blue glow of the intensive care unit lights and the dull, relentless pain in her back and chest.

She couldn't force an answering smile to her lips. "Thank goodness for in-room coffeepots."

Mitch's face grew solemn again and he leaned forward. "What happened, Allie?"

The trembling she thought had washed down the

shower drain returned, and with it the tears. Ignoring her stinging eyes, she quickly and succinctly led Mitch through everything that had happened since she'd found her apartment door unlocked.

"The door was open?" Mitch asked when she finished.

"No, but when I turned the key, there was no resistance. Not enough to notice until I got right up to it."

Mitch frowned. "Sloppy work. What did you think?"

"I was afraid someone was inside. I went back downstairs and got the apartment manager."

He looked thoughtful. "Like any reasonably intelligent person would do, especially someone who knew their life was in danger."

Allie hugged herself. "He was killed in the explosion. I shouldn't have gone to him. I should have called the police first."

"It wasn't your fault."

Allie met his concerned gaze, her eyes welling again with tears.

"Do you know what caused the explosion?"

His methodical, matter-of-fact questions made it easier for her to talk about it.

"I was afraid to wait around, but I heard on the radio something about a gas leak and a lit cigarette."

"There was probably a shorted electrical wire somewhere. Maybe in a light switch. All you'd have had to do was turn on a light. So without knowledge of the unlocked door or the tampering with your cell phone, the explosion could be written off as a tragic accident."

She shuddered. "How did they find me?"

"People often drift into the same habits without thinking about the consequences. Go to the same church, join the same organizations. What did you do during the past seventeen months that you'd done before?"

She brushed her fingers across her cheeks, frowning. "Nothing high profile. I worked. I went to church. Through the church, I got involved with a group of children—similar to the group I formed in D.C. Children who had lost parents or siblings to drunk drivers. Do you think—"

Mitch's gaze held a regretful certainty.

"Oh, my God, I led them right to me." She felt the blood drain from her face. The death of the apartment manager was her fault. That would haunt her the rest of her life.

"Don't beat yourself up about it, Allie. You're human."

"I should have thought about that. Identifying people by their habits was part of my training at Quantico. I was so intent on getting my life back to—normal."

Her voice started out matter-of-fact, but Mitch saw her expression change as she said the word *normal*. She bit her lip, trying to hold back the tears. He knew what she was thinking. The day Joe Barnes was killed, her life had changed. For her, things would never be normal again.

When she'd told him about the explosion, he'd had to restrain himself from reaching for her, to be sure she was whole and unharmed. It was all he could do to keep his voice steady.

"As I recall, you did very well at Quantico. I was surprised you never went on to apply for a special agent position."

She shook her head. "After my father died and I

married Joe, that was as close to the Bureau as I wanted to be."

Mitch winced internally at the reminder of how much she hated the Bureau. "Let me see the phone the Witness Security Program gave you."

Mitch took the phone from her unsteady hand. It certainly wasn't a high-tech piece of equipment. He separated the battery and examined the inside carefully. As far as he could tell, it was the same kind of low-end phone that came with dozens of calling plans. Still, better not to take chances. He broke the plastic case and destroyed the board.

"They couldn't have followed me using the phone, could they? I turned it off."

"There don't seem to be any receivers or transmitters inside it."

She took a breath. "Then how did they trace me to that gas station? *I* didn't know I was going to take that exit until I saw it."

Mitch hesitated. There was only one explanation that fit the facts.

Allie's eyes widened. She'd come to the same conclusion. "I gave you the address of the convenience store on your office phone. Do you think it was tapped?"

"Assuming they didn't tail you all the way from Grand Junction, it's the only logical explanation."

Her face drained of color. "That was Joe's phone. It must be the same people who set him up. Who lied about him meeting that drug dealer."

Her words pierced his insides like a knife. Like the guilt that had twisted in his gut ever since the night Joe was killed. She didn't know. He studied her, wondering how many more shocks she could take. But he couldn't lie to her. Couldn't keep something so vital from her. Not when she'd come to him for help.

"Allie." He touched her terry-cloth-covered knee, just a gesture of support. He didn't allow himself to think about the warm, firm skin beneath the thick white cotton, the skin he had never allowed himself to think about, except in lonely dreams.

He was about to make her hate him.

"I'm the one who testified about the dealer Joe met. I'm the one who followed him that day."

Her face grew even paler, making her green eyes look huge and rimmed with shadow. Her knee under his hand seemed to go cold. He pulled away.

"You followed Joe?" Her voice was brittle, frigid. "It was your testimony that disgraced my husband's memory? That labeled him a crook?"

Mitch flinched at her pain and shock. "I had to tell the truth. I testified to what I saw. Joe met with a small-time dealer that evening, just before he was killed."

She stood, swaying a little, and clutched the edges of the robe together at her throat with one hand. "Maybe the guy was an informant."

Mitch stared at her stiff back, worried that she might faint. He took a deep breath. "Allie, I ID'd him. We had him picked up, and he confirmed that Joe had accepted money to alter evidence."

"He confirmed?" Allie whirled, disbelief marring her even features. "You believed a *small-time dealer* over Joe? Your boss? Your friend? How could you? You knew Joe better than anyone. If he met with that man, he must have had good reason. You don't really believe Joe was involved in corruption, do you?"

Allie bit her lip and watched in growing dread as

Mitch spiked his fingers through his short hair and rose from the bed. He stuck his hands in his pockets and paced, his strong brow furrowed. The black leather of his shoulder holster creaked with his movements. He wouldn't look at her.

Her heart sank to the pit of her stomach. "You *do* believe he was involved."

"I don't know." But he still wouldn't meet her gaze.

Allie's pulse beat a painful staccato rhythm in her temple. If Mitch didn't believe in Joe's innocence, where could she turn? Joe had treated him like a son. "You don't know? Is that all you can say? What did you tell the special counsel?"

"Grant Irby? I gave him the facts. Plain, pure and simple." He straightened and lifted his gaze to hers. "You weren't at the hearing, Allie."

"Of course not. I was supposed to be dead." She had the scant satisfaction of seeing Mitch wince at her words.

"It was clear that they had been watching Joe's activities for some time," he went on.

"Maybe Irby had. He's always wanted to be a special agent. When he took my deposition while I was still in the rehab center, it was obvious from his questions that he would have done anything—even smear Joe's good name—to wrap the case up. You know how many times he's tried for the Bureau. He was always jealous of Joe's rapport with Deputy Assistant Director Conover. I'm sure he feels the same about you, now that you're in charge."

"That may be, but Allie, Joe *was* acting suspiciously."

His choice of words stunned her. Her throat ached.

"Acting suspiciously? What are you talking about?" She shook her head, trying to rid her brain of the meaning behind his words.

But she couldn't. "Oh, dear God, you'd been watching him too. That's why you were so eager to stay with me at the house after dinner that night. You were trying to find out what Joe was up to."

He looked at her steadily, and she read his answer in the deepened lines on his face before he spoke. "I was worried about him."

"Worried? How could you—" She broke off, covering her mouth with her hands. She began to tremble. Collapsing in a chair, she wrapped her arms around herself. Mitch had been the one man she was sure believed in Joe as much as she did. She'd been certain he would help her clear her husband's name.

He stood for a moment, watching her. Finally he said, "You know how much I cared about Joe. But I'm a federal agent. Nothing, not even friendship, can interfere with my job."

Allie squeezed her eyes shut as Mitch turned and left the room, but all she saw was the red and yellow and black of the explosion. She felt just like she had then, as if everything around her had been destroyed. She'd thought Mitch could make everything all right, but he didn't even believe Joe was innocent.

What was she going to do now?

To her dismay, Mitch materialized beside her, carefully balancing two steaming mugs. She looked up, hoping for a glimmer of reassurance, but he wouldn't meet her eye. She'd never known him to evade any question. That he wouldn't look at her terrified her. Was he that convinced of Joe's guilt?

Allie studied her husband's protégé. She'd always thought Mitch was exceptionally handsome in a serious, understated way. He had the rugged good looks of an action-movie star—long, slightly crooked nose, straight, serious mouth and startling blue eyes.

Tall and lean, he moved with an athletic grace that exuded decisiveness and leadership. His brown hair had premature touches of gray at the temples and was cut in a short no-nonsense style that matched his demeanor.

She remembered being surprised at the endearing combination of strength and gentleness with which he'd comforted her during the long, pain-filled hours in the hospital.

She'd thought he too was brokenhearted over Joe's death, and she'd been grateful for his unwavering loyalty to Joe that had kept him by her side until they'd taken her away.

She hadn't known then that he was the enemy.

He handed her a mug and then held out two skinny packets of sugar and a plastic stirrer. She craved the coffee, but she didn't want to accept it from him. However, the delicious smell and the promise of warmth won out over pride, so she grudgingly took the cup.

"That's all the sugar. I know you like at least four packets per cup—"

"You remember how much sugar I like?" She stopped, resisting the sense of familiarity that spread through her at his comment. He was someone who had known her. She'd been so lonely.

"Every time I had dinner with you and Joe, you ordered the richest dessert on the menu, then you'd load your coffee with sugar. It was a wonder you could sleep."

She glanced up and caught a rueful smile playing about his straight, firm lips. As soon as their eyes met, he blinked and looked down at his mug.

But she saw that he was thinking about that last night before the shooting, when they'd sat together in her kitchen and drunk coffee. His presence that night had been so comforting. Now as she thought back, she realized his concern about Joe's absence and his casual conversation must have been his skillful and subtle way to pump her for information. She'd been too worried and too grateful for his company to tell him that Joe probably wouldn't show up until dawn.

There had been too many times like that in those last weeks before the shooting. Too many times when Joe would come in looking worried and tired, just in time to shower and get to work. He'd said he was getting close to a break in her father's unsolved murder case. She'd had no reason to doubt him then, and none now.

She glared at Mitch. "Don't try to make conversation with me," she snapped. "Supposed friendships can't interfere, remember?" She'd made a mistake in coming here.

He sat on the edge of the bed in front of her chair and wrapped his fingers around his mug, ignoring the handle. His hand was in her line of vision. It was a lot larger than hers, with long fingers. It was a strong hand. She shivered. He was wrong about Joe.

"He was a good man, Mitch. He was so proud of his job, so dedicated." She lifted her head and met Mitch's clear blue gaze. "What do you think he was doing that night? Did you know that he devoted a part of every day of the eight years we were married to my father's unsolved murder? About once a week, he'd fill me in on what he'd found out. Many weeks he had nothing to report, but that never stopped him."

Mitch's fingers whitened around his mug. "Your father? You think Joe's death is connected to your father's?"

"Yes, I do. When Joe came in that morning after you left, he told me that he might have some important new information about my father's case by the end of the week." She spread her hands. "He'd told me that before, but this time was different. There was an attitude of—excitement, or anticipation. Maybe the man he met had information about my father's death."

"Do you know who he met that night? Did he ever talk to you about his informants? Ever mention any names?"

"No. He said I'd be better off not knowing any specifics. He always tried to protect me."

Mitch nodded, his eyes on his mug. He didn't believe her.

"Damn it, Mitch Decker," she snapped. "Joe deserved your loyalty."

He looked up then, and she was surprised by the sadness in his eyes. "He had it, Allie. But I had to tell the truth."

"You told the *facts*. You didn't know the truth." He wouldn't help her. If she was going to find the truth behind her husband's murder, if she was going to ever be able to live without fear, she'd have to do it on her own. The loneliness of the past months weighed on her.

But there were things Mitch could tell her, things she couldn't remember. Things she had missed.

"I didn't get to go to his funeral," she said softly, and saw his fingertips tighten again around the mug. "Was it—"

"It was a fitting service for an FBI agent. The director was there. The investigation didn't start until afterward."

"Oh, I'm so glad." Her eyes stung. "The FBI owed him that honor."

Mitch rubbed the back of his neck. "Yes, they did."

His calm agreement angered her. She lashed out.

"You got Joe's job," she spat, not even trying to mask the accusation in her voice.

He looked up, his blue eyes wary. "That's right. How'd you know?"

"We had newspapers in Grand Junction. I tried to keep up with anything having to do with the Bureau."

He nodded.

She looked at the man her husband had loved like a son, and whom she thought had felt the same way. He was remarkably fit and handsome, with his broad shoulders, the hard line of his jaw, the sprinkling of gray at his temples. He was thirty-six; ironically, it was the same age Joe had been when she'd married him. Joe had told her a lot about Mitch, including his strained relationship with his father.

"He wanted you to follow in his footsteps." Her voice was softer than she'd intended.

His mouth quirked up, just barely. But then he immediately grew solemn again. "Just not quite so soon."

As his words echoed in the silence, he stood and walked over to peer out the window. Joe's death hovered like a ghost between them.

Allie followed him. "You knew Joe. You worked with him every day." She reached out and laid her palm against his chest, just above the leather strap of his holster.

"I need an answer from you, not from Special Agent Decker. I want to know what you believe here, in your heart."

Allie's touch seared through Mitch's clothes and into his skin like a brand. He brushed her hand away and stepped past her. How could he explain how many times he'd questioned himself, how many times he'd gone over what he'd seen and heard that day, trying to examine every word, every nuance?

She put her hand on his forearm and he winced, but he didn't have the strength to pull away again. Her touch felt too good. So he stood still and bore it, savored it, for the few seconds it lasted.

Her damp, tangled hair reflected the light like beaten copper, and her eyelashes were wet and spiky. He tried and failed to stop his brain from picturing her lithe, perfect body hidden by the loosely tied terry-cloth robe.

Allie straightened. "I have to find the truth. I have to get my memory back somehow." Her mouth twisted. "No matter what happened that day, I know Joe was not betraying the Bureau. He would never do that. If you won't help me, I'll have to prove it on my own. The very fact that Joe's killer worked so hard to find me tells me there's something missing in the *facts*."

Mitch had to acknowledge that she had a point. He gritted his teeth. Allie had come to him when she was targeted because Joe had trusted him. In a pensive moment, his boss had asked him to watch out for Allie. Mitch had given his word. He would keep it.

"Allie, I swear on my life that you can depend on me. But I can't promise that what we discover will prove Joe's innocence. All I can promise is that we'll find the truth."

Allie shivered and crossed her arms under her breasts. "The truth. That's all I'm asking."

Despite his determination, Mitch's eyes followed the curve of terry cloth to where it parted, leaving the graceful slope of her neck bare.

He forced himself to turn back to the window that looked down on the street entrance of the hotel. His car wasn't out there. He'd parked in the basement of the parking garage. He thought about their situation, about who could be after her. It was dangerous enough if the murderer was a drug lord. If it was someone with connections inside the Bureau, then their danger was quadrupled, because someone inside the FBI had the ability and the technology to anticipate Mitch's moves.

Two flashlight beams crossed in the dimly lit loading area below. He went rigid as he followed the beams back to their origins. Two dark-clad men prowled among the parked cars. They could be cops, or they could be the same two men who had shot at Allie. He muttered a curse.

"What is it?" she asked. "Do you see something?"

"We need to leave."

She stared at him. "Who do you see?" She uncrossed her arms and the oversize robe gaped, revealing a hint of her perfect creamy breasts. He wasn't strong enough to resist a split-second glance before he forced his gaze up to her face, and realized she'd seen him looking at her body.

Her eyes met his, and she clutched the robe together at her throat. For an instant there was a look in her eyes. If she were anyone else—if *he* were anyone else—he might have thought it was a look of hunger, of sexual attraction. He might have thought she was responding to his own poorly hidden yearning. But she was his boss's wife.

He clamped his jaw. "Come on. Our friends from the gas station may be downstairs." He gestured toward the window.

Allie's face blanched. "How did they find us?"

"Followed my car, maybe. Or they could be just working their way through hotel parking lots. I can't be sure it's them, but I don't want to take any chances."

She nodded. "I'll get dressed."

"No. Leave everything here."

She stared at him in surprise. "My clothes? My purse? You think I'm carrying a tracking device? I thought you'd decided it was you who'd been followed."

"I don't want to take any chances."

"But the hotel's robe—"

He almost laughed as he gripped her arm. "It won't be the first one they've lost. Now let's go. We'll take the service stairs."

Chapter Three

Allie looked at the meager array of clothing items she'd just dumped on one of the two beds in the seedy hotel downtown, several miles from the four-star hotel where they'd first stopped. Mitch had whisked her out a back exit and into his car as she'd struggled to clutch the robe around her nakedness.

When he'd gotten in the driver's side, she'd insisted that he stop and buy her something to wear.

He stared at her as if he'd forgotten how she was dressed, and the look on his face confused her. It held equal parts of frustration, surrender and something she wasn't willing to put a name to. Something that burned white-hot and made her fists tighten around the neck of her robe and her thighs tighten in surprising response.

It was the second time he'd looked at her that way. The first time, when his gaze had slid from the open throat of her robe up to her face, it had taken her a fraction of a second to admit that she recognized the feelings his sharp blue eyes evoked. She hadn't experienced a sexual response in a long time. All she'd had room for inside her for the past seventeen months had been grief, fear and a suffocating sense of apprehension that had effectively crowded out most other emotions.

That she would feel such a strong bolt of awareness for Mitch astonished her. She'd admired his strength and grace. Certainly she'd noticed his clean-cut good looks, but she'd never thought of him that way. She'd been married, and he'd been her husband's employee and friend. More important, he was FBI.

For that reason alone, if she'd had any other choice she wouldn't be sitting here beside him now. She wanted her life back.

No. Not *her* life. She wanted a new life, one that was free from the danger cast by the shadow of the FBI.

All those thoughts crowded into her head before she dragged her gaze away from his sharp blue eyes. She swallowed and looked out the window, but her skin still felt touched, caressed, by his gaze.

At the discount store, he'd made her go in with him, refusing to let her out of his sight. Even though it was midnight and the store was nearly empty, Allie was embarrassed to be walking around in public in nothing but a terry-cloth robe and slippers.

She kept one hand holding the robe together and didn't look at the smattering of late-night shoppers as she quickly grabbed a couple of T-shirts, a pair of jeans and a lightweight zippered jacket, along with a few pairs of underwear.

With Mitch urging her to hurry, she'd reached for the first bra she'd seen in her size.

Mitch had picked up toothpaste, toothbrushes and a comb. He was checking out when she remembered shoes. She ran back for a pair of Birkenstock knockoffs and a large cloth purse and returned to find him holding bags and handing cash to a young male clerk, who gazed at her with obvious curiosity and lust.

Now in the cheap, dingy hotel room that seemed to be a study in varying shades of mud, her eyes threatening to glaze over with exhaustion, she stared at what she'd bought.

Mitch came out of the tiny bathroom.

"Sleep in your clothes," he said shortly. "I'll sit up."

"You don't think we're safe here either?"

He shook his head. "It's my training. I'm conditioned to think in terms of danger, not safety. And for all I know those two could have seen us exiting the parking garage." He pulled out his cell phone and glanced at the display.

"But if your car had been reported, wouldn't someone have contacted you?"

He nodded. "I'd have thought so."

"So we're okay for now and you can sleep, too."

His mouth tightened into a straight line and his eyes darkened as he looked at her. She felt like he could see right through the robe.

"Go put some clothes on, Allie."

Feeling rebuked, Allie stuffed everything back into the plastic bag and took it into the bathroom. The tub was dingy, and the corners of the tile floor were black with grime and mildew. Grimacing, she hurried to dress and get out of there.

There was barely enough room to turn around in the little space between the toilet and the bathtub. She hung her bag on a hook on the back of the door and dug in it for the underwear she'd bought. The panties were bikinis, white cotton—not the type she usually wore, but serviceable.

When she pulled out the bra though, she gasped. She

didn't remember it being red lace. *Red.* What had Mitch thought when he'd placed this piece of froth on the conveyor belt?

The red bra dropped from her hands as she dug in the bag without hope. Of course there wasn't another one. She slid out of the robe and picked up the ridiculous little piece of crimson lace, looking at the tag.

"Glamour-Bra." *Great.* The perfect lingerie to run for your life in.

She ripped off the tag and put on the bra. The upper half barely covered the aureoles of her nipples. Feeling heat suffuse her face, she quickly dug out the T-shirts.

"Oh, no," she whispered. They were both white. One was plain, the other sported a colorful butterfly on the front. But when she donned the butterfly shirt, the red bra shone through the cotton like a testament to Erin Brockovich.

She took a deep breath and squeezed her eyes shut. What was the matter with her? She was running from a killer. She didn't have time to worry about what color bra she was wearing.

She pulled on the jeans and jacket, zipping the jacket to hide the bra, and came out of the bathroom. At the rust-stained sink, she quickly brushed her teeth, washed her face and combed out her tangled hair. Without styling spray to restrain it, her hair tumbled in loose waves around her face. She tried to tame it with damp fingers, but without much luck.

She looked at herself in the mirror, seeing a shiny nose, eyes that testified to almost no sleep in two days and hair that slid over her face whenever she turned her head.

It was a good thing she had her Glamour-Bra, she thought wryly.

Mitch glanced out the window of the cheap hotel. There was a lot of traffic on the street below, but nothing that looked out of the ordinary. He checked the time, hesitated for a brief moment, and then punched his boss's cell phone number.

After several rings a deep voice answered. "Yeah?"

"Conover, it's Decker."

"What is it?"

Frank Conover's voice sharpened. The deputy assistant director for criminal investigations knew Decker would never call him so late if there weren't a problem. Mitch had never done so before.

Boy, was Conover going to be surprised. After careful consideration, Mitch had made his decision. As much as he hated to trust Allie's life to his instinct, he couldn't shake the feeling that her enemy was closing in on them.

Joe and Allie had known the person who had shot them. Allie had opened the door without hesitation. The fact that she had known the killer well enough to let him in was an ominous sign. That, plus Mitch's increasing certainty that his office phone had been tapped meant that their attackers must have connections inside the agency.

He'd hurt and frightened Allie. But he couldn't lie to her. Although he'd have sworn on his life that Joe Barnes was a decent man, the drug dealer's testimony and Joe's actions pointed to his involvement with the criminal underworld.

Mitch wiped his face wearily. It had killed him to find out that the man he'd admired so much had been on the side of the criminals.

But no matter what the reason was for Joe's death, the important thing right now was to ensure Allie's safety. The only way he could do that was to hide her until he could find out who had targeted her husband and was now targeting her. And he had the perfect excuse to do so without attracting undue attention.

"Sorry to bother you so late, sir," he said when his boss answered. "When you offered me two weeks off for my father's funeral, I know I told you I didn't need that much time."

"Yeah?" Conover sounded mildly impatient. He obviously didn't consider Mitch's personal leave an urgent matter that needed to be discussed after midnight.

"Well, I'm going to need that extra week after all."

There was a pause, no more than a second or so, but Mitch felt it stretch through his already taut nerves. Then almost before Mitch could wonder about it, Conover spoke.

"I think that's a good idea." Conover's tone had changed from impatience to approval. "Is O'Hara still in charge?"

"Yes. I'll notify him of my plans, sir."

"Where are you now?"

Mitch realized Allie had come into the room.

"Almost to the airport," he said noncommittally.

"So you're flying back to San Francisco?"

Mitch hesitated. He didn't want to tell an outright lie if he could help it. "I still have some family issues I have to deal with."

"Fine. Take all the time you need. Get some rest." Conover cleared his throat. "I'm—sorry about your father. Do you know when you'll be back?"

"Not yet. I'll give you a call. Thank you, sir." He cut the connection and considered his deputy assistant director. Conover hadn't mentioned Allie's disappearance from the Witness Security Program, although Mitch was certain he'd been notified. Of course, Conover had no reason to disclose such confidential information to Mitch.

"Mitch, is everything okay?"

He realized he'd been staring at his phone and shifted his attention to Allie. Her face was shiny and pretty, and her lithe body was gracefully sexy in the tight discount store jeans.

It was going to be a challenge to be this close to her and maintain his professionalism, but he had to do it. He didn't trust her life to anyone else.

He needed to notify his staff that he'd be gone a few more days. And if he was going to keep Allie safe and find out who wanted her dead, he was going to need help.

He called a trusted member of his team—Jack O'Hara.

FRANK CONOVER GLANCED at his cell phone, which displayed the number of his newest special agent in charge. Mitch Decker was one of the most trustworthy, dedicated agents Conover had ever met. He was loyal, protective of his staff and an idealist who believed in right and wrong. For Decker, there were no gray areas.

For that reason alone, he'd never make it any higher than special agent in charge, Conover thought cynically.

Joe Barnes had been different. Joe had understood that occasionally choices had to be made, choices that weren't always easy to explain. But that was the nature of the job. Joe understood the gray areas. He could have had a future.

But then Joe had chosen Decker as his protégé. Joe should have known Decker didn't have the necessary qualities. He'd chosen Decker for personal reasons. It was obvious he'd felt a fatherly love for the young, promising agent. It was admirable, but the wrong way to go about choosing a successor.

Now Joe was dead. Frank shook his head slightly and slipped out of bed. His wife murmured something.

"Nothing, sweetheart. Go back to sleep."

Frank went downstairs to his study and closed the door. He wouldn't sleep any more tonight. He set his briefcase on the desk and opened it. There were two files inside, one thick, the other slim. He leaned back in his chair and picked up the thinner file.

The signs had been there, even before Joe's death. Decker was turning out just as Conover had predicted he would. Idealistic. Romantic. Honorable. He reminded Conover of Harry MacNeal, Allie's father. The former deputy assistant director had been incorruptible. Ironic that MacNeal had chosen Joe, and Joe had chosen Decker.

Conover pulled out the transcript of Allison Barnes's deposition and turned to the page he'd already read several times.

DEPOSITION OF ALLISON MACNEAL BARNES IN THE MATTER OF THE MURDER OF JOSEPH LEROY BARNES GRANT IRBY, ESQ. EXCERPT

Q: Mrs. Barnes, what is your relationship with Mitchell Leeds Decker?

A: Special Agent Decker is a member of the Division of Unsolved Mysteries. He works— worked—for my husband. They were friends.

Q: Isn't it true that you and Special Agent Decker spent the night alone in your home on the night of January fourteenth of last year?

A: No! It is not!

Q: Special Agent Decker's deposition confirms that he did not leave until 3:00 a.m.

A: That's not the same as all night.

Q: Why don't you tell us what he was doing there?

A: Joe and I were having dinner with Mitch at Chez George when Joe was called away. He asked Mitch—Special Agent Decker—to take me home, and he did.

Q: Why did Special Agent Decker stay until 3:00 a.m.?

A: Because he knew I was worried.

Q: He knew you were worried. So he stayed to— what? Keep you company?

A: (Witness pauses)

Q: Wasn't it because this was not the first time your husband had been gone all night?

A: Yes.

Conover read the last part again. Decker had stayed with Barnes's wife until three o'clock in the morning the night before Barnes's murder. Conover asked himself the question that had plagued him all these months.

Why had Decker been there? Had he and Barnes's wife lied about what had happened between them that night? Had they discussed anything that might lead to Barnes's killer?

Maybe Decker wasn't as honorable as he appeared.

He reached for his cell phone and dialed his assistant, Stanley Sherbourne. Sherbourne's sleepy voice answered on the fourth ring.

"Decker just called me on his cell phone. He's taking a few more days off."

"Yes, sir?" Sherbourne's voice sharpened.

"Have someone check flights. D.C. to San Francisco."

Conover heard bedclothes rustling as Sherbourne got up.

"You don't think he's leaving, do you?" Sherbourne's voice was tinged with excitement. "You think he's—"

"I'm not sure what he's doing," Conover said pointedly. "But whatever it is, I want you on top of it. Understand?"

"I understand. I'll take care of it, sir."

Conover cut the connection. Sherbourne was good. All the people working for him were. Conover had gotten to where he was today by carefully choosing his people, then letting them do their jobs.

He looked back at the deposition.

He hadn't chosen Decker.

ALLIE LISTENED as Mitch talked to Jack O'Hara. He told Jack he wouldn't be in the office for a few days, and asked him to contact an undercover cop named Dan Withers, and have Withers obtain some unmarked cash and find them a place to stay. He also gave Jack the three numbers from the dark car's license plate, and told him about the vehicle sideswiping his car.

"Pick up my car and have any paint deposits collected and run," he said, then listened. "Okay. I'll call you on your wife's phone when I need you." He turned off his cell phone and rolled his shoulders.

"Mitch?" She walked over to him, wanting to reach out, touch his shoulder, ease his tension. He'd just buried his father. Was that why he looked so tired? Why his face was grimmer, his eyes sadder than she remembered? "I'm sorry. About your father."

He nodded, glancing at her, and then away. Somehow his brief glance made her want to retreat. It was filled with a very private pain. If she could wipe it away, she would.

But there had always been something distant in Mitch's manner. Something formal. Except for those few times she'd woken in the hospital to find him beside her. It could have probably just been the medication or their shared grief, but she'd felt so close to him, so comforted and protected, then.

"I'm sorry," she repeated, retreating to her bed.

She sat cross-legged on top of the covers and watched him as he stood and slipped out of his jacket. His black leather shoulder holster stood out in stark contrast to his white shirt, reminding Allie that he might be helping her, but he was also a part of the reason she needed help.

"For some reason, I thought you'd already lost your dad."

Mitch's jaw tightened visibly. "I did. A long time ago." He dropped onto the other bed without removing his holster, and stuffed both pillows behind his head.

The irony in his voice reminded her of Joe's description of Mitch's estrangement from his father. "Was it sudden?"

He closed his eyes and grimaced. "Yeah. A stroke. He was in the middle of negotiations to buy a foundering software manufacturer."

"So he was into software?"

"No, he was into money and power. He bought companies in trouble, restructured them, usually at the expense of hundreds or thousands of jobs, and then sold them." Behind the flat words Allie heard the hurt and betrayal of the boy whose father hadn't been a hero.

So that was why he had become so close to Joe. Joe was the father Mitch had never had. A man he could look up to.

"How did you end up in the Bureau?"

"I guess I wanted to do something good. To help people, rather than destroy them."

A short laugh escaped Allie's throat. "So you chose violence? In my experience, the FBI is pretty good at destroying lives, too."

Mitch pulled himself up to one elbow, his face grim, and his eyes burning with blue fire. "I swear to you, Allie, I won't let anything happen to you. I'm working on a way to get you to safety."

"If that's what you're doing, you're wasting your time. I spent seventeen months in *safety*—" her voice made a mockery of the word "—while other people were supposed to be looking for Joe's murderer. Well, in all that time, nobody caught the killer. When my apartment blew up, none of the people who were supposed to be keeping me safe came to my rescue. If it's all the same to you, I'd feel safer out searching for answers."

"Allie—"

"If it's someone connected to the FBI who killed Joe, how can you or anyone else protect me?"

"By hiding you where he can't get to you."

Allie shook her head. "And when you don't know who the killer is, how can you know who to hide me from? No. I'm through hiding. There's only one way I can really be safe, and that's to recover my memories of what happened that night and bring those people down."

"I agree. But until you remember, you're vulnerable. I need to make sure no one knows where you are."

"Then why did you tell Jack O'Hara about me?"

"Jack can help us. He can keep me informed of what's going on with the police and with the Bureau."

"And you trust him?"

"I trust Jack with my life. And yours." Mitch's voice was steely, his face grim. "I'll be calling him using his wife's cell phone, and he won't talk to anyone."

"And Frank Conover? You didn't tell him you were with me."

"Conover thinks I'm taking the personal time he offered me for my father's funeral. If he knew I was helping you, he'd be obligated to report me."

"But you didn't tell either of them where we are."

"I thought it better not to." Mitch pinched the bridge of his nose as he made the ominous statement.

Allie knew how he felt. Exhaustion lay over her like a heavy blanket; beyond the exhaustion was a dull ache in her back and an empty queasiness she recognized as hunger. Despite her worry, she couldn't stifle a yawn.

Mitch shot her an appraising look. "It's been a long day. When was the last time you slept? You need rest."

"Shouldn't we be planning our next move?"

"Tomorrow." He reached over and turned out the lamp, blanketing the room in darkness.

Allie stretched out cautiously, adjusting the pillow under her head. But she was wide awake. She didn't like being shrouded in darkness by the dingy room. It made her feel as if there were crawly things hiding in the shadows.

"I haven't slept well since it happened," she said to the darkness. "Whenever I close my eyes, I see my hand reaching for that doorknob."

There was no response for a few seconds, although she heard Mitch's quiet breaths, feel his attention riveted on her. "And that's all? You don't remember opening the door?"

"I don't even remember turning the knob. The therapist the WSP made me see told me the reason I can't remember is because I would have to face that it was someone I know who murdered Joe and tried to kill me."

"Who?"

The stark question sent a shard of panic stabbing through Allie's chest. She laughed uneasily. "That's the sixty-four-thousand-dollar question, isn't it?"

"Who can you name who might have wanted Joe dead?"

Allie sat up and pulled her knees to her chest and hugged them. She stared at the opposite wall, considering Mitch's question. "I've thought about that so many times. It's such an impossible question. Everyone liked and respected Joe."

"Even Joe must have had enemies, particularly in light of the dangerous types he knew. What about that agent who was selling information?"

"Seacrest or Scagrest? Something like that? About four years ago? He threatened everybody."

"Right. Tom Seacrest. He said he knew where everybody in the Bureau lived and he'd gun us all down as soon as he got out of prison."

"I never saw him, except for a newspaper photo. Didn't they put him in a psychiatric facility?"

"He should still be in prison, but I'll get Jack to check on him. Who else?"

"Irby, of course. But I hardly think he'd be capable of murder. Besides a couple of other threats from people Joe had put into prison—" Allie shrugged.

"What about Carmine Bongiovi?"

She looked up at him. "Carmine Bongiovi? I don't think Joe knew him. I think the person who killed Joe is the same person who killed my father." She tightened her grip on her knees.

"You mentioned that earlier. The official stance is that your father was killed by one of the two warring families in the city. Either Bongiovi or DeSanto. Right after your dad's death the power began to shift away from DeSanto and to Bongiovi."

"Joe told me all that." Allie sighed and rested her cheek on her knees. "But I've never even met Bongiovi, so why would I have let him in? Irby told me that all the physical evidence indicated that I knew the person, let him in voluntarily. So we're back where we started."

"Not quite. Weren't you supposed to be out that night?"

"It was a Wednesday, so I normally would have been at the Community Outreach weekly staff meeting. But I hadn't slept the night before, and I was worried about Joe. I wanted to be there when he got home."

She heard the bed creak as Mitch got up. "Who knew you were gone on Wednesdays?"

"Anybody who knew me. There had been a recent series of articles in the *Post* on drunk driving, so anyone who had taken the time to find out would have known that my program for children affected by drunk driving was part of the FBI's Community Outreach Program."

"We know you opened the door. And now we know whoever was at the door wasn't expecting to see you. We know Joe couldn't have been home more than about an hour when the doorbell rang. Between the time I saw Joe get into his car and the time the informant I was following stopped at that bar was not quite an hour and a half."

"Mitch, tell me what you saw that day."

There was silence for a long time, punctuated by unexplained rustling and creaking. She wrapped her arms more tightly around her legs.

"Joe left work early," Mitch said. "Something he never did. Before he left, he stopped by my desk."

Mitch paced in front of the small window that reflected red and yellow from flickering neon signs. "He thanked me for staying with you the night before."

"I'd told him you'd stayed. He said that was just like you." She paused. "He told me if I ever needed anything, I should come to you."

Mitch's hand brushed through his hair and down to rub the back of his neck. He turned toward her in the dark, his lean frame distorted by the silhouette of his shoulder holster. "When I asked him to give you my best, he just nodded. He seemed distracted."

"Why did you follow him?" she asked.

Mitch sighed. "I knew something was wrong. I wanted to make sure he wasn't in trouble, to be there if he needed help."

Allie's skin prickled with apprehension.

"He drove to a discount store where he met with an informant. They argued. I couldn't hear all of it but Joe finally yelled that he wouldn't change his mind. Then Joe left."

I'm not changing my mind. Joe's voice echoed in Allie's head. When had she heard him say that?

"I followed the informant. As soon as I saw him using his cell phone, I got an uneasy feeling. When he stopped at a bar, I immediately called 911 and turned around and headed for your house."

Allie's hand tingled as her only memory of that night flashed before her inner vision for the hundredth or the thousandth time. Her hand reaching for the doorknob of the front door of her Georgetown home to let Joe's killer inside. "How did you know?"

"I'm not sure." He paused for a long moment. "Instinct."

Allie wondered why he spat that word as if it tasted like gall. "If you had waited another minute to call 911, I'd be dead."

Mitch cursed. "I will never forget you lying on that cold tile floor in all that blood."

The horror in his voice told Allie how thankful she should be that she didn't remember being shot. His eyes glittered in the darkness, and she knew he would never forget it. "Joe didn't have a chance, did he?"

"No. Whoever shot him stood right in front of him."

Allie put her palms to her temples and squeezed. "I must have let the killer walk past me and up the hall toward the kitchen. Right up to Joe. And then I was shot in the back."

"You were shot in the back because you had the presence of mind to dive for the phone. Many people would have rushed toward their spouse."

Anguish and regret choked her. And stuck in a knot

in her breast was the question—could she have done more? Could she have saved her husband? She put a hand to her throat.

"You couldn't have saved him." Mitch's voice was tight, and she knew he'd asked himself the same question she had.

"But you're wondering if you could have."

He made a restless movement. "We'll never know, will we?"

Allie wanted to say something comforting, but she couldn't deny the truth of his question. They would never know.

"Allie, what did Joe tell you?"

So he was back on track. Brief regrets over. Searching for the truth.

She closed her eyes. "Joe came in at dawn that morning, a couple of hours after you'd left. I had gone to bed, but I wasn't asleep."

"What did he say?"

"I waited, but he didn't come upstairs. So I went down." Joe had been sitting at the kitchen table where she and Mitch had sat, clutching a mug of coffee, his face ashen, his manner brooding.

"He was in a strange mood. Worried, shaken, but at the same time—" she spread her hands, searching for the right word "—confident, as if he'd made a decision."

Mitch sat up. "What decision? What did he tell you?"

Allie massaged her temples tiredly. "I told you, he was excited about some new information in my father's murder case." She spread her hands. "But he'd told me that before."

A deep, familiar sadness spread through her. She missed Joe and her dad.

"What else?"

"I don't remember anything else," she snapped. "I told Grant Irby everything I remembered."

"Is what you just told me in your deposition?"

Allie thought about it. "I don't think so. Irby didn't ask me anything about the night before, except to make insinuations about you being at our house. I guess Irby is still handling the investigation?"

Mitch nodded. "The local police have jurisdiction. And the DEA is involved, because of the informant Joe met."

She reached over and turned on the lamp. "No offense, Mitch, but I hear crawly things in this room."

Mitch blinked in the sudden light. He couldn't help the ghost of a smile that twitched his lips at the sight of Allie hugging her knees, as if she could keep the bugs and vermin away by sheer force of will. She was strong. He'd seen that in the hospital. She'd fought death and conquered it. Crawly things didn't stand a chance.

"Sorry about the accommodations."

Allie smiled wryly and her knuckles whitened as she squeezed her knees even more tightly. She looked straight at him.

"So what now?"

"Allie, my primary concern is protecting your life. My identification of the punk Joe met earned us nothing but a small-time dealer. The real criminals are still out there. I need to get you back into the Witness Security Program."

Allie shook her head. The Witness Security Program hadn't helped her recover her memories, nor provided the safety it had promised. She knew she would never be safe until she remembered, until she could identify the man who had shot her.

"I told you, that's not going to happen. You're not getting rid of me that easily. What you need to do is help me dig the memory of what happened out of my brain. The sooner I can remember, the sooner the slime that killed Joe and tried to kill me can be put away. Then Joe's name will be cleared and I can live the rest of my life and never think about the FBI again."

Mitch sent her an odd look. "We'll talk about that tomorrow. Right now we need to turn out the lights and get some sleep."

Her stomach protested. "If it's all the same to you, let's leave the lights on. But I don't think I can sleep until I get some food into my stomach. I'm so hungry I'm shaking." She needed nourishment and rest, in that order. Then she and Mitch could figure out how they were going to retrieve her memories, whether he wanted to help her or not.

"I haven't eaten since early this morning—or yesterday morning. Think this place has vending machines?"

Mitch nodded. "I saw some downstairs in a room off the lobby. I'll go grab some stuff. What do you want?"

"I don't care." She smiled sadly. "Just so it has calories."

MITCH PUSHED another quarter into the slot, then punched a button. Potato chips. Not very nutritious, but they'd do until morning. He thumbed more change into the machine and sprang for some cheese crackers.

It was typical of what he knew about Allie, that her concern was not for her own safety. She'd come to him because she hadn't known who else to trust. And she was making a simple request. Help her regain her memories and find Joe's killer.

A bolt of pain pierced his heart. He wanted the person who'd murdered Joe as much as she did. If he could, he'd have already found the bastard and locked him up.

Allie didn't know he'd spent the last seventeen months trying to answer the same question that plagued her.

What had been bothering Joe? What had he known that had gotten him killed?

Mitch had done some investigating on his own, but before he'd gotten anywhere, he'd been called on the carpet by his boss, and reminded that he was on probation in his new job and that there was an official investigation into Joe's death. Conover had told him there was plenty to keep him busy at the Division of Unsolved Mysteries without sticking his nose into an investigation that was not his purvue.

As he slid a dollar bill into the soft drink machine, he heard heavy footsteps pounding up the wooden stairs.

Then a crash.

He dropped everything and ran, drawing his weapon. He took the stairs three at a time. His heart stopped when he saw the door of their room gaping open.

"Hey! Hold it!" he shouted, his gun pointed at the door. A shot from inside ricocheted off the door facing, narrowly missing his shoulder. As he flattened against the wall, a heavy body shoved past him and hurtled toward the stairs.

Mitch fired. The figure tripped and rolled down the stairs.

Had he hit him? He didn't have time to check.

He angled around the doorway of their room. He'd heard more than one set of footsteps.

His vision suddenly filled with black as a human missile body-slammed him and dove for the stairs.

Mitch flipped onto his stomach and fired, taking a chunk out of the banister.

Regaining his feet, he flew downstairs after the second attacker, shouting at him to halt, but the man made it out the front door and into the open passenger door of a dark car.

Mitch burst out onto the sidewalk in time to catch a glimpse of the vehicle in the light from the hotel. From its bullet-riddled exterior, he was sure it was the same car as earlier. He fired at the window, then at the tires. One tire blew. The car nearly spun out, but the driver compensated.

As the car whipped around a corner, a shot rang out, whizzing past Mitch's head and thudding into the brick wall behind him.

Mitch ran, hoping to get off another shot or a better look at the license plate, but the crippled car was too fast for him. Not willing to waste another second, he rushed back into the hotel, past the panicked desk clerk and up to their room.

It was empty.

"Allie!" he shouted, panic screaming through him, his weapon still held in readiness. "Allie!"

Where was she? Was she safe? His heart crashed against his chest wall.

"Mitch?" Allie cracked open the bathroom door, then stepped out. Her face was ashen, spots of color burning high on each cheekbone. "Are you okay? I heard gunfire."

Relief clogging his throat, Mitch holstered his weapon and crossed the room in one stride. He grabbed Allie's shoulders, sharply assessing her. "Are you hurt?"

"No. No, I'm fine." She strained against him. "You're squeezing my arms."

"Sorry." He let go. He'd been so damn scared. His head had been filled with a horrifying vision of her bleeding on the floor again.

"I shouldn't have left you alone." He took a deep breath and surveyed the room.

They'd obviously watched him leave, then kicked the door in. Thank God the vending machines were right next to the stairs.

Splintered wood peppered the cheap brown carpet. The pillow Allie had been hugging lay crosswise on the bed, a bullet hole marring its surface. His imagination fed him a freeze-frame of Allie lying there, the bullet hole in her chest.

"I heard them on the stairs and ran into the bathroom," Allie said shakily, following his gaze. "I jumped into the tub when they started shooting."

Mitch dragged his gaze away from the pillow. "Quick thinking."

He studied the boot print on the door and the broken lock. Their pursuers had found them—again. And this time, Mitch knew they couldn't have tracked Allie.

Allie voiced the question that was running through his mind.

"How do you think they found us this time?"

He shook his head. "They must have followed us from the other hotel, or they triangulated on my cell phone signal."

Her sharp gaze met his. "If they know your cell number, doesn't that prove it's someone connected to the Bureau?"

"It's possible someone outside could obtain that information, but not likely."

Mitch surveyed the room as he talked, but their attackers had left almost no evidence. "We've got to get out of here. Go underground."

Allie stared at him. "You can't do that. What about your job? The division?"

"Jack O'Hara is in charge now. The division couldn't be in better hands."

Her hand touched his arm, preventing him from turning away. "This isn't like you. Your first priority has always been your job. Your career will be ruined."

She was right. His job had always been everything to him. It bothered him that she knew him that well. What she didn't know was that there was one thing that meant more to him than his job, more than anything.

He couldn't meet her gaze. His eyes burned with bitter grief. He'd failed to save the man who'd thought of him as a son. He wouldn't fail him again. Anything was worth the risk, including his job, if it ensured Allie's safety. He'd gladly die if his death would give her the chance for a normal, happy life.

He shot her a quick, hard glance. "I promised Joe I'd take care of you."

Chapter Four

Allie followed Mitch out of the hotel and into the pre-dawn darkness, slipping out an alley door just as the police drove up. She heard the desk clerk's excited chatter punctuated by lower, calmer voices as Mitch's strong arm circled her waist and pulled her around a corner.

"Do you know this area?" She wrinkled her nose at the hot, nauseating smell of garbage and wished she had tennis shoes or boots instead of the fake Birkenstocks as she stumbled over foam containers and garbage bags trying to keep up with him.

"I used to, when I worked undercover." He pulled his cell phone out of his pocket, separated the battery from the case, and threw them in opposite directions down the alley.

He grabbed her hand and urged her forward. "Come on. They'll canvass the area. We've got to get as far away as possible."

They ran for a long time as the sky slowly lightened. Allie had to rush to keep up with Mitch's longer stride. By the time he slowed to a stop, she was gasping for breath. Mitch was huffing, too.

He wiped his brow with his forearm and caught her arm. "You okay?" he asked.

She nodded, glancing around. They were in a part of D.C. she'd never been in before. Old buildings with faded signs hinted at a better time. Monster-mouthed broken windows yawned, the jagged glass gleaming like sharp teeth.

"Where are we?" she asked, instinctively moving closer to Mitch's protective bulk as she searched for a street sign.

"R Street. There are several homeless shelters in this area."

"Homeless shelters?"

Mitch nodded. "An undercover cop I know is going to find us a place to stay."

Allie looked around. The sun was just rising, its light creeping into the shadows, exposing people huddled in alleys and lying in doorways. This was where Mitch thought they'd be safe?

She shuddered, and to her surprise, Mitch wrapped an arm around her and pulled her close.

Bending his head, he whispered, "Hang in there, Allie. I promise I'll get you to a safe place." He gave her a reassuring squeeze before he placed his hand on the small of her back.

"I'm fine. What now?"

"We've got to blend in, so we have to do some work. Follow my lead."

Allie relished the reassuring feel of Mitch's hand on her back. She'd lived in D.C. all her life but she had never been this far down R Street. It was a different world. She'd grown up steeped in the Bureau, but her father and her husband had sheltered her. She hadn't realized how much.

How different would her life have been if she'd followed through with her training and become a special agent? How much more prepared might she have been to deal with this unknown threat? And the biggest question—could she have saved Joe?

They passed sleepy-eyed people on the street. Worn-out hookers in tight miniskirts shuffled along barefoot, swinging their four-inch heels by the straps. Young men walked home two and three abreast, swaggering and talking loudly, showing off their baggy clothes and ballsy attitude.

Mitch spotted the building he'd been looking for. It looked like a vacant storefront. He shoved the door open and pulled Allie inside, into a bare, musty room lit by a single naked bulb.

As he'd expected, before they'd gotten two steps into the building, a gaunt black man who stood at least six foot five stopped them in the doorway. "Yo, dog. Not so fast."

The man barely glanced at Allie before pinning Mitch with a calculating glare, but Mitch didn't miss his appraisal of her small diamond-stud earrings.

He hated exposing Allie to such danger and squalor, but until he could get her to a safe house, he had to protect her the best way he knew how.

"What's up, Fred?"

The man took a step toward Mitch and Mitch felt Allie's body go rigid. "Who—hey. Is that you, Dixon?"

Mitch nodded, his hand brushing Allie's to reassure her. "Yeah. Dixon." Dixon had been his undercover persona.

He smiled when the other man's street talk changed to cultured, perfect diction. Frederick Scarbrough, known as Scarecrow, had an MBA from Brown University. After his daughter and wife were killed in a senseless shooting at a bank, Fred had opted out of his upper-middle-class job and drifted into the life he now lived, as the proprietor of a crack house. He'd been a valuable asset to Mitch when Mitch worked undercover.

"I wondered if you'd still be here. How've you been?"

The black man grinned, showing a mouth full of perfect white teeth, but Mitch saw the lingering sadness in his eyes. "Man, I'm doing fine. Business is good. What about you? You disappeared after that sting operation. I had to cultivate a whole new set of friends. What was that—six years ago?"

"Probably seven by now. I took a different job."

"Oh yeah? I'm thinking about the same thing. This—" he waved a large, skeletal hand "—gets old after a while. Besides, even though renting rooms is not illegal, I know that eventually some overzealous police officer will decide to make an example of me. So I want to move on while my record is clean."

"Good for you, Fred. What are you thinking of doing?"

"I might fix this place up and sell it. People are looking to renovate this part of town."

There was a noise behind Fred.

"What you want?" Fred's voice stretched into a whine as he slipped back into street vernacular. He tilted his head almost imperceptibly and sent Mitch a warning look.

"Just looking for information." Mitch held up his hands, following Fred's lead.

"I might happen to know connections if you looking

to score. I got bunks. I ain't got no drugs, and I ain't got no information." The man took a step toward Mitch.

Mitch didn't back down. "I need to trade some jewelry for clothes that are a little more appropriate to the neighborhood."

"Ain't got nothing you or that bit—"

"*I said—*" Mitch stepped toward Fred, stopping his words "—I've got jewels. You've already checked them out." Mitch glanced at Allie, who was watching, wide-eyed.

"Let me have your earrings, babe." He jerked his head and snapped his fingers. "Now!"

She jumped at his tone. He winced internally, hating to treat her with disrespect, even if it was a ruse acted out for whoever was listening on the other side of the door. To her credit, Allie removed the earrings without question and handed them to him.

He held out the diamonds to Fred. "Clothes?"

Fred sent him a knowing look. "I'll see what I can do. Y'all come on inside." He gestured toward an inner door.

"We'll wait here."

"Tha's your choice." Fred disappeared through the door, and Mitch heard him speaking in a low voice to someone.

"Mitch, what are you doing?"

Mitch waved his hand in a silencing gesture. During his days undercover, he'd helped Fred and Fred had helped him. He hoped he could depend on him now. He'd like to question Fred about the talk on the street, but Fred's actions made it clear that they couldn't talk freely.

Mitch's first concern was to camouflage Allie and

himself so they could blend into the background. Especially Allie. Her distinctive red hair and soft, cultured voice were going to be hard to disguise.

All Mitch had to do was roughen his tone and say little. With different clothes, a few days' beard, and his undercover training and experience, he knew he could slip seamlessly into the street life, because he'd done it before. But Allie's very bearing telegraphed to anyone who saw her that she didn't belong in this world and never would. Mitch wasn't sure how he was going to successfully hide her.

Fred reappeared, with a handful of dingy, wrinkled clothes. He tossed the stuff at Allie.

She caught them without flinching.

"Can we change in here?" he asked Fred.

"Sure can." Fred propped his long, lanky body against the wall.

Mitch ignored him and started to take off his coat.

"Say, that's a fancy piece you got there."

Mitch stopped. For some reason Fred felt the need to stay in character, but Mitch didn't like him mentioning his gun.

"How 'bout I take it off your hands?"

Mitch stood up straight and stared him in the eye. "How about you go on back to what you were doing? We'll leave our clothes here for you."

"How 'bout I call the police? 'Cause it looks to me like you two are runnin' from something."

Mitch shrugged.

Fred nodded toward Mitch's left wrist. "Well, then, how 'bout that watch?"

"What for? You said you don't have any information."

Fred's black eyes narrowed. "Did I say that? Maybe I was wrong." He swaggered over to the interior door and looked around it, then turned his head and raised his eyebrows. "Step into my office, dog."

Mitch assessed him, then jerked his head at Allie. "Come on."

She followed them without a word, but her eyes sparked.

Fred led them through the room, down a hall and into another, smaller room that was dark and furnished only with a scarred table and two straight chairs. Fred sat behind the table and pushed a pile of papers aside. Mitch noticed some real estate ads in among the pile.

Mitch gestured for Allie to sit in the chair but she declined. She stood in front of the door, clutching the bedraggled clothes to her chest.

Mitch stuck his hands in his pockets.

"We can talk in here, Dixon." Fred's street whine was gone.

After a quick survey of the room, Mitch looked at Fred. "You know anything about a guy called Hangout?"

"Hangout Hooper? Yeah, man. Used to own a dive across town. That's where he got his name."

Mitch played with his watch, unclasping and clasping the band.

Fred's eyes followed the movements of Mitch's fingers. "Heard he drew a nickel for dealing, then made a deal with the Feds. Got something for nothing."

"You could say that." Mitch unclasped his watch. Hangout, the man he'd seen Joe talking to that fateful day, hadn't even known Joe was FBI, or so he'd said when they picked him up. By identifying Hangout, all

Mitch had given the Bureau was a small-time dealer. All Hangout had gotten was parole.

"I hear he's sellin' over on Sixteenth. Small-time ounce man. Not like the old days."

"Sixteenth." Was that all Fred knew? "What about the street? What's the word—"

Behind Allie, the door opened. She jumped, and slid over next to Mitch. He put a casual arm around her and pretended to kiss her ear and cheek as he checked out the intruder out of the corner of his eye.

"Yo," Fred said, his limbs suddenly turning to rubber as he lounged back in his creaky chair. "Dat door was closed."

A short dark man with bad teeth spoke rapidly in Spanish. Fred sighed and answered in the same language, then gestured.

The short man grunted and left.

"And close it," Fred called.

When the door clicked shut, Fred sat up and drummed his long, skeletal fingers on the rough desktop.

"Hangout likes to take his meals at a place called Moe's."

Mitch raised a brow. "Moe's?"

"Hey, I didn't name it."

"Thanks, Fred." Mitch slid the Rolex off his wrist and tossed it to the man. His father had given the watch to him when he'd graduated. It didn't matter. "Take care of yourself, you hear?"

"Don' worry about me, dog." Fred grinned, but his eyes stayed sad. "I'll leave you and your lady in here to change. Then you can leave the way you came in."

Mitch nodded. Fred disappeared through the door.

Allie's eyes were wide and troubled. "Who's Hangout?"

"Not now," Mitch said quietly. "Let's see what you've got there." He grabbed what looked like a drab coat from Allie's hands. He held it up. It had once been a suit coat, but it was limp and grimy now.

Mitch shrugged out of his jacket and removed his shoulder holster. He unbuttoned his white shirt and looked at Allie, who eyed the clothes she held with distaste.

"What else?"

Allie's hands were shaking. "Um, there's a short black skirt and a baseball cap." She sorted through the items. "A T-shirt that must have been used to wipe up something I don't even want to think about. A dirty pair of jeans. And these."

Mitch suppressed a smile. *These* were a pair of silver shoes with very high heels and nothing but slender little straps to hold them on.

"Put on the skirt and the shoes."

Allie stared up at him in consternation. "What's wrong with what I have on?"

"Those pants are so new they shine. Too obvious. You can keep your butterfly T-shirt. We'll rub some dirt on it as soon as we get a chance. The red bra showing through it will be a good effect with that little skirt and those heels."

Her face turned bright pink. "A good effect? What effect are you going for, the hooker look?"

He shrugged, suppressing a wry smile and a heavy ache in his loins. If she knew how much torture he'd gone through since she'd donned that bra, her face would be as red as the lace.

She lifted her chin, swallowed, then unbuttoned her jeans. He grabbed the man's jeans and turned his back. He was well aware that they were both likely being watched, but he wasn't going to tell Allie that. He would give her at least the illusion of privacy.

He dropped his pants and pulled on the jeans. They were slightly short and tight. He looked down at his brand-new Loafers with regret. It wouldn't take more than a couple of minutes of concentrated work to age them by several years. He put on his shoulder holster over his T-shirt and donned the jacket. It was too big, which was good. It would hide his gun.

Turning, he caught Allie tugging at the bottom of the skirt.

She looked down at her shoes. "I can't walk in these," she said.

Mitch swallowed and prayed for restraint. The mini-skirt barely hit her mid-thigh. He had never seen more than a few inches of Allic's forever legs, although he'd dreamed about them. They were as creamy smooth as he'd imagined and the shoes emphasized her slender ankles and shapely calves. His mouth watered.

The T-shirt came to just below her slender waist, and gave a delectable hint of the perfect breasts encased in red lace. Her hair had dried into corkscrew curls that tempted him to plunge his fingers into them.

"Do I look as slutty as I feel?" she asked with a hint of a rueful smile in her voice.

You look sexy as sin. Mitch didn't say what he was thinking. He would never say that to her. His job was to protect her. He owed that to Joe. To her.

Allie couldn't interpret the expression on Mitch's face. All she knew was that his intense blue gaze sent a lightning bolt of desire streaking through her. For one thrilling instant, all her fear and anxiety were swept away in a liquid surge of erotic longing that frightened her with its ferocity.

She stared at his profile, at the tiny bump in his otherwise straight nose, and the determined line of his jaw. What was the matter with her? She shouldn't be attracted to Mitch Decker. He was everything she *didn't* want. He lived and breathed FBI. He probably didn't even take Christmas off. The attempts on her life and the stress of no sleep and no food were getting to her—that was all.

Mitch took her hand. His grip was warm and comforting, and not even his determined scowl doused the new, disturbing feelings inside her.

They exited the building and headed down the street. "Put on the baseball cap," he commanded her. "That red hair is like a flag."

She jerked her hand away from his and defiantly twisted her hair up and stuck the cap on her head. His commanding tone and curt orders were like a slap in the face after the instant of awareness they'd shared.

"You know, I'm not one of your agents," she snapped, knowing he was right, but irritated at his abrupt change of manner.

"That's true, you're not." He didn't even acknowledge her with a look.

"Don't patronize me. I've had training."

He paused briefly. "I'm sorry, Allie. But we've got to act the part if we're going to blend in around here. Just let me do the talking." He stalked ahead of her.

Act the part. Of course. She looked down at herself. Even though she was dressed appropriately for her role, she knew she was sorely miscast. She teetered on the three-inch heels. But she'd have to learn now.

She studied the streetwalkers and the girls who huddled in the corners of buildings. Lost, frightened kids and women with no hope. They shared one thing. In their haunted eyes was a bravado that didn't quite mask their hopelessness and despair.

Mitch stopped at a cross street and leaned one shoulder against the graffiti-covered wall of yet another abandoned building, but he didn't relax. The curve of his back was deceptive. He looked like he was slouching carelessly, but his gaze missed nothing, and his hands were loose at his sides. He was balanced, poised, ready for anything.

The baggy jacket didn't hide his lean strength. The two days' growth of beard didn't detract from the harsh beauty of his face or the sharpness of his blue eyes. But to a casual eye, he looked like a guy down on his luck, possibly an addict.

He was good.

He kicked nonchalantly, rhythmically, at the wall and the sidewalk. For a few minutes Allie watched him, wondering what in the world he was doing. Finally, she understood.

He was deliberately scuffing his shoes. She stood beside him and tried to imitate the tense stance and wary expressions of the girls she'd seen.

After Mitch's shoes were scraped and dull, he bent and ran his hands around the grimy edge of the building's wall where it met the sidewalk, then straightened and looked at her. "Come here."

He grinned wickedly, a sexy, come-hither look like nothing she'd ever seen from him before. His gaze, deliberate and slow, traveled from her face down her neck to her breasts. His frank appraisal filled her with pulsating awareness all the way to her very core. Her breasts tightened and her nipples scraped against the lacy cups of her bra. She swallowed nervously.

His brows lowered and a muscle in his jaw clenched. He'd seen her body's reaction.

That knowledge caused her nipples to ache with the need to feel his lips, his tongue. Her breasts felt heavy and full. Her breathing grew shallow.

"Come here, Allie. Play along. Act like we've spent a wild night together and we don't want to have it end." His grin widened and he held out his hand.

Her gaze flickered to the front of his tight jeans, where the faded denim traced the enticing outline of his arousal. Her breath caught. She blew air through her pursed lips and raised her eyes to his just as someone brushed past her on the sidewalk.

Mitch reached out and grabbed her.

"What are you doing?" she protested, laughing uneasily. "Your hands are dirty."

"That's the point," he said in her ear, pulling her close, but not close enough. "Act like a hooker. Pretend you're enjoying my groping. I'll be done in a minute."

Pretend. She bit her lip as he ran his hands over her shoulders and down the front of her T-shirt. His palms slid over her sensitive breasts, sending desire sparking through her. But he didn't linger there. He immediately ran them down and around, his palms skimming the edges of the two scars in the middle of her back.

Unable to control her wobbly knees or the deep thrill coursing through her, Allie rested her cheek against his shoulder.

He rubbed her back then slid his gentle, caressing hands around her waist and up, to the underside of her breasts. "There. Now you blend in a little better with the homeless people and the two-bit hookers."

He straightened and let her go.

Still caught up in the new, disturbing sensations his hands had evoked, she almost fell against him. Her hips brushed his. Just as she felt the hard length of his arousal against her belly, he gripped her shoulders.

"That's enough," he whispered.

She could have cried. His sexy grin, his caresses, had been just for show, an excuse to get the dirt and grime on her shirt. He'd had one purpose in mind, camouflaging her.

But she'd also heard the ragged edge to his voice. Mitch Decker might be the consummate professional. He might be helping her because he'd made a promise to Joe, but he wasn't indifferent to her.

She should be grateful for his restraint, not disappointed, not angry with him for stirring feelings in her that she'd never felt before.

He sidestepped her, his eyes hooded by his dark brows as he gave her T-shirt a clinical appraisal. "Now we wait for my contact. Try to make yourself comfortable." To illustrate, he slouched against the wall once again.

People passed them by, most so engrossed in their own problems they didn't spare them a glance. A few sharp-eyed individuals looked Allie over and gazed narrowly at Mitch.

Feeling rejected, Allie cocked one hip and turned away from him, crossing her arms under her breasts. She affected a bored scowl and reached down to adjust a strap on one shoe.

She heard a soft chuckle.

Without looking at him, she propped a fist on her hip. "What?" she challenged him.

"Not bad. You almost look like you belong here."

"Why, thank you, I think." She heard the approval in his voice and it warmed her. "I assume that means you don't think I stick out like a sore thumb in this getup."

"Not like a sore thumb," he murmured, his gaze traveling lazily down the front of her T-shirt over the skimpy skirt, on down to the ridiculous shoes and then back up. His eyes emitted heat like fingers of fire licking at her skin.

She crossed her arms across her breasts, conscious of the red bra showing through the thin T-shirt material.

"You never did tell me who Hangout is."

He closed his eyes briefly, then cocked his head. "Come over here." He held out a hand.

She glared at him suspiciously. "What now? Am I not trashy enough yet?"

His eyes flared with laughter that he didn't allow to reach his mouth. "You're perfect. But you asked me a question, and I don't want to yell."

Allie took two steps and found herself pulled in front of him. He spread his legs and nestled her between them, his hands clasped around her lower back. Trying to look as if she were enjoying his closeness and discovering that it wasn't much of a chore, she relaxed against him as much as she could without giving up the last ounce of her self-control. She saw his throat move as he swallowed and a thrill ran through her.

"Do you do this on purpose?" she asked.

"Do what?" he said, tilting his head to nuzzle her neck, his lips moving against her skin.

She closed her eyes and let her head fall back, unable to resist the feel of his mouth and the gentle scrape of his beard. She tried to concentrate on his words rather than on the seductive brush of his warm, firm lips against the ultra-sensitive skin behind her ear.

"Hangout Hooper is the informant Joe met with that night."

His words stabbed her like so many stilettos. She froze, then pushed against his chest with all her might. For a few breathtaking seconds, she'd forgotten that Mitch didn't believe in Joe as she did.

He met her gaze, his eyes hooded. "I'm sorry, but you asked. I followed him, ID'd him and then watched him get off on probation for a minor drug offense. We never got anything out of him about why they met or who had sent him."

Allie lowered her hands to her sides and stepped backwards. Mitch let her go. She leaned against the building again, and hugged herself.

Mitch turned sideways, propping one shoulder against the wall. "I'm hoping he knows more than he told us."

Allie refused to look at him. "Good," she said coldly. "At least you can satisfy yourself that you're right about Joe being corrupt, even if you don't solve his murder."

Mitch shot her an exasperated look and then closed his eyes again, as if he were trying to nap. Allie reluctantly moved a little closer to him, close enough to feel the heat of his body, telling herself it was because it made her feel safe.

SEVERAL HOURS AND a couple of sodas later, Allie leaned against the building, half-asleep, and wished she knew where to find a clean rest room. The drone of the traffic and the slur of voices echoed in her ears. Beside her, she felt Mitch stiffen, tension emanating from him like a scent.

She roused, her heart pounding. "What is it?"

"Stay cool." Mitch's low voice barely reached her.

Carefully, she settled back against the wall as a slumped figure lumbered toward them. A dingy shirt torn around the tail hung over ill-fitting pants of no discernible color or age. The man's hair was a mat of dreadlocks. He didn't appear to be watching where he was going. Instead, he studied the sidewalk at his feet.

Right in front of Mitch, he leaned down and picked up a cigarette butt.

"Light?" he growled.

From somewhere, Mitch pulled a lighter and lit the butt. Allie took a small step away as the man leaned in toward the flame. She fully expected the man's dreads to catch fire.

"How's it going, Withers?" Mitch said softly.

Surprised that Mitch called the vagrant by name, Allie took a closer look. The man's glance flickered sideways to hers as he puffed on the butt. Bright hazel eyes narrowed in a grimy face as he looked her up and down.

"Good," Withers said, leaning back against the wall beside Mitch, puffing greedily on the butt. "Real good. Hear you need something."

"A place to stay. Clean. Private."

Withers coughed, shook his dreads and wiped his mouth on his sleeve. "Don't ask for much." He coughed again and flung the cigarette aside. "How long?"

"Day or two."

Withers straightened, checking out the street as if expecting to meet someone. "What's the deal?"

"I'm surprised you don't know."

"Assume I don't."

Mitch stared beyond the man. "Can't say."

"Or won't."

Mitch's brows lowered slightly. "Or won't," he agreed.

"R and Fifty-third. Twenty bucks a night, no questions and no bathroom. Cash."

"What's it called?"

"Hayes Rooms. Says No Vacancies. It always says that."

"Okay. What about the other?"

Withers reached a grimy hand into one of his voluminous pockets and pulled out a small wad of cash.

"Thanks." Mitch accepted the cash and stuffed it into his jeans. "Some place around here to get a prepaid cell phone?"

"Sure." Withers hacked again and shuffled his feet, peering down as if he were hoping to turn up a cigarette butt. "Couple of streets that way, on your way to Hayes Rooms."

"Any word on the street?"

Withers shook his head. "Not much. Seems like the Marshals and the Bureau are trying to keep a low profile on this."

Allie watched the entire exchange with interest. A lot of information was shared in very few words. As Withers slunk off, a chill of unease tingled up her spine.

"How do you know you can trust him?" she asked.

He shot her a glance. "There are some chances I have to take. He's a cop. He saved my butt a few years back when it could have cost him his job. Let's go take a look at our accommodations."

LATE THAT AFTERNOON, Special Counsel Grant Irby's cell phone rang. He looked at the caller ID, then got up and kicked the door to his office closed. He'd told Withers never to call him at work.

He pulled a neatly folded handkerchief out of his breast pocket and wiped the mouthpiece. "What?" he snapped.

"*Someone* just reported seeing Decker and Mrs. Barnes."

Irby's pulse sped up and he felt sweat pop out on his forehead. "Together?" What was Decker doing with Allison Barnes? He was supposed to be in San Francisco at his father's funeral.

"Yep."

"Where?" This might be just the break he'd been waiting for.

Decker had always seemed a little too sure of himself, ever since he got the Bureau job Irby had wanted. Mitchell Decker was one of those overachievers who got everything handed to him on a silver platter. Irby had suspected seventeen months ago that Decker and Joe's wife had been more than just friends. Her deposition hadn't changed his mind. After the shooting, Decker hadn't left her side in the hospital. Now she'd run to him.

"Well now, it's difficult to say just exactly where they were."

Anger heated the portly lawyer's neck. "Don't give me a hard time." He blotted his face. "I'm sure the police and the Bureau would be interested to find out that you sell information. You're in a vulnerable position."

"I'm not the only one. You can't do anything to me without implicating yourself."

"You'd be surprised what I can do," Irby said, then sighed. He had to have the specifics, and Withers knew it. "What will it cost me?"

"Ten thou."

"Good God. Don't be ridiculous!"

"Hey, I ain't got a dog in this fight. Take it or leave it. I can get that much elsewhere."

Irby was surprised. "Elsewhere? Who are you talking about? Is someone else on to this?"

"The price just keeps getting higher and higher."

"Where do you think I'm going to get that kind of money? I'm a government employee."

Irby heard a chuckle in Withers's voice. "Yeah. And you buy those suits you wear out of your government salary."

Irby's stomach hurt. "That's enough. Give me a day or so. I'll get the money. Now where are they?"

"My mama didn't raise no fool. You'll find out when I have the cash."

"Call me tomorrow. Early." Irby turned off his phone and stood under the air vent until his anger cooled. He folded his handkerchief, lining up the edges carefully, creasing it just so. He had to think. He was certain Withers had firsthand information. Withers was a lowlife, but his information had always been accurate.

Decker was hiding the only witness to Joe's murder. What a coup it would be if he could prove that Mitchell Decker had murdered Joe Barnes. Irby knew no one would be surprised if Allison Barnes turned up dead. The only reason she'd lived as long as she had was because she'd been hidden in the Witness Security Program. Just not hidden well enough.

It would be very satisfying to see Decker go to prison. That would leave an opening in the Bureau.

Chapter Five

"Oh, Mitch! Oh, it's so good." Allie closed her eyes and made an appreciative sound. She licked her lips as she chewed and swallowed a mouthful of red seedless grapes.

Mitch couldn't keep his eyes off her lips, which were shiny with juice. She would taste like grapes, cheddar and soft, warm woman.

She smiled at him as she reached for another cracker and tilted the can upside down to spray a gob of processed cheddar cheese on it. The grapes were almost gone, and the six-pack of bottled water was down to three.

Mitch chewed on a grape and finished his second bottle of water. He wasn't hungry—not for food. His body tightened in instant response as he watched Allie wolf down the cracker. She wiped a smear of cheese off her lip, then sucked on her fingertip.

His tight jeans were torture as his arousal throbbed. He was disgusted with himself. He routinely warned his team about staying focused on the job and not letting emotions or hormones interfere. And here he was, dangerously close to succumbing to both.

"Do you want more cheese?"

He shook his head and stood, walking over to the hazy window that looked out over R Street, pretending to survey the street below while he got himself under control. All he had to do was think about her lying in her own blood to regain his focus.

Withers had been right. They'd gotten a room easily, no questions asked, although this place was one step above a crack house, and several steps below the seedy hotel they'd fled hours before.

He hadn't missed Allie's hesitation as they walked into the dark lobby that smelled of unwashed vomit and flesh. But with every hour they spent together, his admiration for her grew. She hadn't complained. She'd shown the instinct and good sense of an agent from the moment her apartment had blown up in front of her eyes.

And in that moment, when she hadn't known where to turn, she'd turned to him. But the hurt in her eyes when she'd found out he'd been suspicious of Joe's activities told him she'd never forgive him for not believing in the man who'd believed in him.

The irony was he did believe in Joe. Despite all the facts, his gut told him the same thing Allie had. That no matter what Joe was doing, he'd had a good reason, a noble reason. But he had nothing to base his belief on—nothing but instinct. And instinct, unlike facts, was unreliable.

He scanned the street below, looking for anything odd, anything out of the ordinary. This section was poorly lit, which made it popular with the homeless. In the alley across from the hotel, two sloppily dressed kids were having an argument about something. They separated and took off in opposite directions as a police cruiser drove by.

Inside, through the walls, a woman yelled at a child to shut up. Farther away, the sound of a television or a radio penetrated the silence.

In the dirty window's reflection, he saw Allie turn toward him. Even reflected in the streaked glass, she was beautiful, with her green eyes and all that wavy hair framing her delicate, heart-shaped face. The curve of her back and her drawn features told him how tired she was.

All he could offer her was an eight-by-ten room with one bed and no progress on solving her husband's murder.

He faced her. "You're exhausted. Climb into bed. I'll sit right here."

Allie didn't protest. She just nodded. "I guess I'll sleep in my clothes."

He sat down in the ugly, overstuffed chair wedged between the bed and the wall.

She inspected the bed before climbing in.

"Looking for crawly things?" he asked.

She scowled at him. "Yes. You want to make something of it?"

"Not me, ma'am."

She slid in between the covers and lay her head gingerly on the pillow.

"We could leave the light on."

"No. Despite what you think, I'm not a scaredy-cat."

"I know that."

She reached up and quenched the lamp's light, plunging the room into a semi-darkness punctuated by orange beacons from the gas station across the street.

Mitch slid down in the chair and tried to find a comfortable position. He adjusted his holster so it didn't stab into his side and closed his eyes, but there was no way he was going to be able to sleep, not with Allie so close. How, through all the musty, acrid smells that permeated this dive, could he still smell the hint of lavender and spice that had always been a part of her?

He must have dozed off because a soft noise woke him. He stiffened and sat up, reaching for his gun.

He heard it again. It was Allie.

"Allie? Are you okay?"

She sat up, her wide, frightened eyes reflecting the orange neon wetly. "Oh, Mitch, I'm sorry. I didn't mean to wake you." Her voice sounded small and scared.

He walked around the bed and turned on the lamp. "What's the matter?" Curled up in the bed, she looked like a child, but when she sat up and pushed her hair back, the red bra pressed against her T-shirt, and reminded him that she was all woman.

Allie's face burned with chagrin as she wiped tears off her cheeks with trembling fingers. "I guess I am a scaredy-cat," she said with false lightness, clenching her teeth to stop her voice from quavering. "I tried to relax and I—started shaking, and I can't seem to stop."

Mitch sat next to her on the edge of the bed. "You've had a rough couple of days. You've got a right to be scared."

She clenched her fists, frustration pushing the awful panic aside for an instant. "You wouldn't say that to me if I were one of your agents."

Her glare dared him to contradict her. He didn't say anything, and that made it worse. She knew she was right. Mitch Decker would never excuse such a reaction in a member of his team. Embarrassed, she pressed both hands over her mouth.

"Damn it. I—swore I wouldn't do—this," she sniffed. "I swore I was—going to be—strong." She clenched her jaw, but the tears came—scalding her cheeks, sobs threatening to escape from her aching chest.

Mitch held out his arm, and instinctively, she moved closer, though her brain reminded her that he was the enemy, even as her body sought the shelter of his.

For an instant, he sat immobile, allowing her to hang on to him but not yielding. Keeping that formal distance that she'd always thought was a part of him, until those times in the hospital. But he'd been grieving then. His guard had been down.

His arms closed around her.

With a sigh, she laid her head against his chest and felt the rapid beating of his heart.

"You are strong," he said, his voice rumbling against her ear, his breath stirring her hair. "You survived. You came all this way alone."

She fisted her hand against his chest. "I feel so helpless."

"Shh." His hand caressed her shoulder, then he slid his fingers under her chin and urged her head up.

"Don't cry," he whispered, his thumb brushing across her lower lip.

She felt his lips against her forehead—warm, firm, steady.

"Allie, don't cry."

His familiar, comforting words echoed through the emptiness in her heart, lighting all the dark, scary places inside her. She didn't care if Mitch was only helping her because he'd promised Joe. She only knew that right now she needed something to draw her fears away. She needed him to feed her a bit of the steel that was so much a part of him.

Without considering the consequences, focusing only on the warmth of his lips against her skin, she lifted her head, seeking more.

Unerringly, his lips moved across her temple, down her cheek and over hers, lightly, questioningly.

She moaned in response.

He bent his head, his mouth covering hers, his tongue sliding along her parted lips and farther, exploring the inside of her mouth.

He whispered her name as his fingers slipped up her nape and through her hair to cradle the back of her head as he deepened his kiss, invading her mouth in an erotic prelude to lovemaking. The sensuous stroking of his tongue sent shivers of desire down to where all her sensation was centered.

She kissed him back greedily. His mouth looked so hard, but felt so seductively supple. She breathed in his scent, felt the rough stubble of his beard scrape her cheek and chin. He was all male, deliciously solid and strong.

She reached up to pull him closer, hungry for more of the breathtaking sensation of being wrapped up in him.

He stopped.

Stunned, Allie tried to hold on to the feelings, but Mitch turned her loose as if her skin had burned him.

"Damn," he rasped, his voice ragged with emotion. His jaw worked as he stood, his back stiff. She saw his throat move as he swallowed. "I'm sorry, Allie."

Allie pushed back against the rickety headboard, her limbs still shaky, now with desire rather than nerves, her own breaths sharp and short.

"Sorry? For what?" She pulled her legs up and hugged her knees, feeling abandoned. She shouldn't have given voice to the question, because she wasn't sure she wanted to know the answer. What was the emotion that roughened his voice? She peered at him. Was he really sorry for the kiss, or sorry that he'd lost control? "For comforting me when I needed it?"

Comfort was an inadequate word for what he'd given her. And it was the wrong word for what she'd sought. She'd wanted proof that there was someone she could count on to beat back the fear, to stand with her against the invisible foe she fought. Someone who was alive and strong and dependable. She wanted the assurance she'd felt when she'd awakened in the hospital and found him there, guarding her. She wanted the feelings his touch evoked in her.

She should have been the one to pull away, but his strength was too seductive. Passion still swirled inside her as she watched him regain control over his emotions. She wished she had that much discipline.

He lifted his head and shrugged his shoulders, as if to release the tension there. Then, without looking at her, he turned toward the window.

"It won't happen again. I promise." He stood silhouetted by the ugly orange light, his manner formal, his words distant and entirely professional.

Allie closed her eyes, amazed at how much his words hurt. He was sorry for the kiss. "I know."

Mitch cursed himself silently but fluently as he clenched his jaw and forced his breathing to slow. How had he let that happen? As he'd promised her, it wouldn't happen again. Her life depended on his self-control.

He searched inside him for the strength to face her dispassionately.

"Allie," he said tightly. "Your safety is my responsibility. If I'm going to protect you, you're going to have to help me. It's understandable that our enforced closeness and the tension level we're experiencing might stir a need for release. It happens. But we have to resist that impulse."

He stood and looked down at her, his expression grim. "We can't let our guard down, not for a minute. It could get you killed."

Mortification flooded her face, making him regret his curt tone and harsh words. "I'm aware of the danger, Mitch."

"I know you are."

"And I understand that you're just reacting to tension and the fact that I'm female."

"That's not—"

Allie held up a hand. "I agree. We're together out of necessity." She slid off the other side of the bed, using it to put distance between them. "I just wish we were both working toward the same goal."

"I know you don't believe it, Allie, but we are. Now you need to sleep."

Rationally, she knew he was right. They had to stay focused. She'd learned that in her own short time in training. The FBI instilled professionalism, focus and loyalty in its agents.

Loyalty. Her lips curled wryly as Mitch withdrew, physically and emotionally. He sat down in the threadbare chair not three feet from her, but she felt more alone than she had during the months she'd spent in the Witness Security Program.

Mitch might have lost his focus for an instant, but now the steel was back. Her brain knew that his strength was what she needed. Someone wanted to kill her, and Joe had told her she could trust Mitch.

But her heart wondered. She hadn't imagined his response. He wasn't unaffected by her. But when it came down to it, where would Mitch's loyalty lie? It was as if he were two people. Joe's protégé, who'd promised Joe he'd take care of his wife, and the career FBI agent, dedicated to finding the truth, no matter what the consequences.

Which man was the real Mitch Decker?

SOAKING UP the morning sun beside his pool and sipping Jamaica Blue Mountain Coffee while reading the *Sunday Washington Post* was one of Carmine Bongiovi's favorite pastimes.

Giggles and squeals floated over to him on the morning breeze as he turned off the cell phone and set it down.

"Daddy, watch!" He looked up in time to see his six-year-old daughter jump into the wading pool in a blur of dazzling blue swimsuit and bright yellow water wings. She splashed water everywhere. His wife, sitting on the steps of the pool, ducked the spray and laughed as she trailed the baby's toes in the water.

"Did you see me, Daddy?"

"I saw you, Bambino." He forced a smile for his little girl, as he silently cursed the double-dealing piece of scum who'd spoiled his morning.

Carmine Bongiovi valued loyalty. He provided efficient service, and he expected the same. His business had always depended on his good name.

Withers was playing both sides, and Bongiovi knew it. He'd had the undercover cop on his payroll for years. Withers was useful, up to a point. This morning, he'd come very close to overstepping that point. Still, he was the only link Bongiovi had to Allison Barnes, now that she was in the wind with Decker.

And Bongiovi needed Allison Barnes. So he had no choice but to play Withers's cheating game. For now.

He took another sip of coffee, sighed and punched a number into his cell phone.

"Yeah, I need ten thousand in small unmarked bills. I *know* it's Sunday."

A breeze picked up the corner of the business section of the *Post.* Bongiovi grabbed for it with his free hand, and it tore as it blew away. He cursed.

"How the hell should I know?" he yelled into the phone. "Ain't that what I pay you to figure out? Just get it."

Bongiovi turned off his phone. His daughter chased the newspaper that had blown away.

He smiled when she brought it to him, the big yellow wings dwarfing her little arms. "Thank you, *principessa.* Run along now. Papa is busy. After a while I'll come catch you while you dive."

She leaned up on tiptoe to give him a wet, chlorine-scented kiss.

As soon as he had Allison Barnes's location, he'd be able to set the events in motion that would eliminate his problem. All his problems.

Of all the jobs he'd done himself and all he'd ordered done, this one was by far the most important and the most dangerous. But he was doing it for the best of reasons—his daughters.

He set the business section aside and picked up the front page.

MITCH HAD BEEN awake since sunrise. He hadn't slept well. His dreams had been filled with erotic visions of sea-foam-green eyes, lavender-spiced skin and kisses that almost took him over the brink.

He'd woken up with a painful arousal that he'd tried to ignore. But this time, not even thinking of Joe and Allie sprawled on the floor like marionettes dropped into spilled red paint had tamped his desire.

He was tempted to dispose of the problem quickly and alone, but he quashed that thought almost before it had formed. Not only was the idea pathetic, it demonstrated an extreme lack of willpower. Much like the lack of willpower he'd exhibited last night.

Allie had been through too much in too short a time. It had been bound to have an effect on her. But that didn't excuse him from crossing the line he'd sworn never to cross. She was his boss's wife.

So he'd paced up and down the unlighted, smelly hallway outside their room until he finally had his emotions in check.

He'd carefully avoided looking at Allie, sweetly sleeping, when he'd come back into the room. He'd crossed to the window and watched the sun come up and the street people start to stir.

A police car drove by, and Mitch followed its progress until it was out of sight. He didn't know if the police were looking for Allie and him, but he wouldn't have been surprised.

He checked the time indicator on the prepaid cell phone. It was late enough to call Jack.

He stepped back out into the hall and punched in Holly O'Hara's number. Jack answered.

"Just for the record, I'm getting Holly a new phone."

Mitch allowed himself a small smile. "Good idea. What do you have?"

"Nothing from forensics on the break-in and shots fired. The desk clerk accurately identified you. He wasn't so sure about Allison."

Mitch sighed in wary relief. "That's good. How'd they know which room?"

"The desk clerk finally admitted that a young black male had been hanging around, asking about a white couple."

"No ID, I guess. Okay, what about my car?"

"Our friendly special counsel had it impounded. Natasha pulled up the police report on the forensic evidence. No paint."

"No paint? I saw it. It was metallic black. Right front fender. Tell her to check again."

"I already did. No paint."

Mitch cursed softly.

"Yeah," Jack agreed. "What you said. Somebody got to the car. Now it seems to me there are only a few folks who could do that."

Mitch let his silence speak for him. Jack was smart enough and careful enough to come to the logical conclusion, and if it came down to it, he'd be able to truthfully say he and Mitch hadn't discussed any involvement by local law enforcement or the FBI in tampering with evidence in a murder case.

"Nat's also narrowed the partial license and your

general description of the car to about ninety-three possibilities. We're going over them."

"Let me know. What about ballistics?"

"Same song, second verse. Holes in the car. Inconclusive. No bullets recovered. I'm working on something."

"Jack, don't put yourself or the team in jeopardy over this."

"No, sir."

"How're they doing? How's Eric?"

"They've picked up a suspect in the rape case he was profiling. The perp was right where Baldwyn said he'd be. That kid is spooky."

"Yeah. Keep an eye on him. He forgets to eat. Everybody else?"

"Everything's fine here. Your team knows you. They're not worried."

Mitch gave a short, harsh laugh. "That's good. I am. Is Storm still out?"

"Nope. Got back yesterday."

"Good. Keep everybody close."

"Conover called. He knows you're out there. He's declared you AWOL and on suspension pending an investigation, even though you told him you were taking leave. If you don't show up by tomorrow, he's going to put out an APB."

"I'm not worried about that."

"You're risking your career."

"Let it lie. Now, what about you?"

"Don't worry about me."

"Jack—"

"Conover's already grilled me. I told him the truth. I don't know where you are. I could receive an official admonishment for not informing him that you'd called me. No sweat."

"You're out of the loop after this call."

"The hell I am!"

"That's an order."

"Sorry, Decker. You're not in charge now. I am."

Mitch cursed.

"I checked your office phone. Didn't find a bug, but I dusted your desk and door. Got a bunch of nice prints. Probably five or six different sets. I'm having Reese run them. If the phone was debugged after you got Mrs. Barnes's call, then maybe we'll find a print that's not on the authorized entry list."

"Good. Thanks."

"Oh, the Marshals are calling too. Apparently they'd like to talk to you about Mrs. Barnes's whereabouts."

"Tell them to get in line."

"Already did. What's your plan?"

"I don't have a plan."

"That's not like you, boss."

"Yeah, I know. Until Allie can remember who she saw that night, her life is in danger. I'm not taking any chances. So we're staying hidden for now. If you hear anything, call me. Oh, one more thing. Remember Tom Seacrest?"

"Are you kidding me? Everybody remembers him. Threatened to kill every agent in the D.C. area. He's still in prison."

"Make sure. I don't see how he could be involved, but see who his contacts are. See if he could have ordered Joe killed. And find me a way to get Allie to a safe house in complete anonymity."

"That'll be a trick. Everybody's looking for her."

"My number one priority is keeping her alive, and she's too exposed out here. Everything would be easier if she was out of the way."

Mitch realized Allie was standing at the door. Her eyes glittered in the dimness. She'd heard him. He only hoped she'd heard everything and not just the last bit.

"Got to go."

"Any message for Conover?"

"Nope. Don't give him anything. Keep it close, Ice Man. I don't know who is behind this, but I can't afford even the smallest leak. It could be anybody. *Anybody.*"

Mitch turned off the cell phone and ushered Allie back into the room, closing and locking the door behind him. He glared at her. "What the hell were you doing opening the door?"

"When I woke up, you weren't here. And I have to go to the bathroom."

"So you were just going to walk down the hall alone? Don't ever take a chance like that again. You don't stick your nose outside this room unless I say so."

Allie propped her fists on her hips. "Then don't leave me alone without telling me where you are."

Her eyes were damp, but they snapped with anger. She lifted her chin and straightened to her full five feet eight inches of height.

"I won't. You can trust me on that. I need to be able to trust that you won't forget for one minute that you are the target of a killer who may have the highest level of resources behind him. I will not take even the smallest chance with your life."

Allie's face crumpled and she crossed her arms, withdrawing into herself. "I know that. I appreciate everything you've done."

It seemed he was destined to frighten and hurt her. His instinct was to reach out and hold her, but holding her wasn't practical or logical, even if it was what he wanted more than anything. He cursed under his breath.

"Mitch, I'm sorry about last night."

"Last night?" He pretended to double-check the lock. Not for the same reasons he was, he'd bet. Not because he'd had a taste of her spicy sweetness and for the rest of his life, he'd be haunted by knowing the exact flavor of what he could never have.

"About breaking down. It won't happen again."

He looked at her then. At the determined angle of her chin, the set of her delicate jaw and the slight puffiness around her eyes. She was frightened and brave and beautiful, and Mitch didn't know if he had enough strength to keep her safe from the killer and from himself.

He nodded briskly. "I know it won't. You're doing fine."

"What do we do now?"

"I need to check in with Fred, see if he's heard anything, and go try to find Hangout. You stay here. Keep the door locked and I'll leave you the cell phone."

"I'm going with you."

"That's not a good idea."

"Well, I'm not staying here alone. This is my fight, and if you think I'm going to sit around here like I sat in Grand Junction, doing nothing, you're wrong."

Mitch scowled and held out the cell phone. "If anything happens, you can call Jack."

Allie stood in front of Mitch, her chin in the air, determined to stare him down if that's what it took. "I'm going with you."

"No. You'll be safe here."

"You didn't think so five minutes ago when I stuck my *nose* out the door. I thought you trusted your cop friend who got you the room."

"I don't trust anybody completely, except a few of my staff."

"I guess that puts me in the *anybody* category."

Mitch's eyes darkened. "I trust you. You should know that. But right now, neither of us can trust your memories. I'd like to know that if we saw Joe's murderer out there, you'd be able to ID him, but you can't. Not yet." He checked his holster. "But he'd know you. That's why I don't want you out in the open."

"Well, I'm not staying here."

"If I'm going to be able to protect you, you've got to do what I say."

Allie blew out an exasperated breath and spread her hands. "You have got to be the most stubborn, single-minded man I have ever met. I never asked you to protect me. I asked you to help me find the truth."

She looked at her open hands, and thought about how powerless and vulnerable she'd felt when the men had come crashing up the stairs and broken into their room during the few minutes Mitch had been gone to the vending machines.

She didn't have to be helpless.

"Mitch, I need a weapon."

Chapter Six

Allie watched as Mitch blinked and started to say something, shook his head, then stopped and looked at her narrowly.

"Don't even think about saying what you're thinking. I've been through Quantico. You've seen me at the range with Joe. You know I can handle a weapon. My father taught me, and Joe made sure I kept in practice. Joe had me go through requalification a few months before—before he died. I passed."

Planting her feet, shoulders' distance apart, she crossed her arms, staring straight at Mitch, daring him to say something sexist.

He surprised her.

"You're right." Propping a scuffed Loafer on the edge of the bed, he rolled up the leg of his jeans and unbuckled a small, sturdy ankle holster. "Here. Are you familiar with a SIG Sauer?"

"Yes." Allie removed the weapon from its holster, glanced at the safety, ejected the magazine, checked it and slapped it back into place.

The glint of admiration in Mitch's blue eyes almost made up for his rebuff.

She tucked the gun inside the cheap cloth purse she'd bought at the discount store, within easy reach.

"Thank you," she said with a grateful smile. "This makes me feel better. Now, we're going to Fred's?"

Mitch glowered at her as he shrugged into his jacket. He pointed a finger at her. "You do not do anything unless I tell you to. You don't talk, you don't even squeak. Understand?"

"Is this how you talk to your team?" she asked smartly, as relief washed through her in waves. She really hadn't wanted to be left alone. And while she'd been quick to tell him she wasn't looking for his protection, the idea of being separated from him for even a short while made her uneasy.

He shook his head as he checked his weapon. "None of my team would dare question my orders."

If she weren't looking at his scowling profile, she might have thought there was a note of amusement in his voice. "Really? That's not what I've heard. You have a reputation of respecting each team member's strength, and rarely order anyone to do anything." As she spoke, Allie hefted her purse, checking its balance with the weight of the little gun.

"I have a highly trained, exceptionally competent team who have proven they know when to talk and when to keep their mouths shut. Now stick all your hair up under that cap and pull the bill down so it shadows your face."

"Yes, sir." Allie bit her lip to keep from smiling as she did what she was told.

Out on the street, Mitch tucked his chin down into the collar of the jacket and stuck his hands in the pockets as he shuffled along the sidewalk.

Allie slipped her hand into the crook of his arm, following his lead as they passed curled-up lumps of color and shadow that turned into sleeping people as morning dawned. Mitch kept his eyes straight ahead, so Allie did the same, not looking anyone in the eye, not the hookers, not the hungover kids trying to find their way home, not the street people stirring and groaning at the prospect of another hopeless day.

Even at Mitch's shuffling pace, Allie had trouble keeping up in the silver high heels. She stumbled over a crack in the sidewalk and cried out when her toe banged into a pebble.

Mitch wrapped his arm around her waist, still scowling. "Try to stay upright, okay? And stick close to me." His voice was stern as he guided her through a line of bedraggled men outside a homeless shelter, waiting for breakfast.

Allie bristled. "I wouldn't be having this trouble if you hadn't made me wear these shoes." She leaned against his shoulder and spoke teasingly, seductively. "When we get to your friend's place, Baby needs a new pair of shoes."

His head snapped up. She smiled and shrugged. A reluctant grin tugged at his straight, firm mouth and his gaze slid down her legs to those ridiculous high heels.

"It's a deal," he said gruffly.

Several blocks later, as the sun peeked over the dingy buildings, Mitch guided her across a street and into the abandoned store where they had gotten their clothes.

By the time he closed the door, the tall, gaunt black man was there.

"Yo—hey. Whassup, Dixon? You and your lady are up early."

Mitch's knuckles scraped his chin. "Look again, Fred. It's not that early. You must have slept late."

"Naw. You putting old Scarecrow on the wrong side of the day. I ain't gone to bed yet. So, *Dixon.* I been hearing talk."

"Yeah?" Mitch raised his brows. "Like what?"

Fred glanced behind him and then came through the door into the dimly lit front room, leaving his Scarecrow persona on the other side of the door. "I understand there are a lot of people looking for an agent named Decker. Say he's gone rogue."

Allie's hand tightened on Mitch's arm. He didn't react. "People?"

"An undercover cop we both know. Goons working for Carmine Bongiovi." Fred assessed Mitch. "And Bureau men."

"Bureau men? What Bureau men?"

Fred shrugged. "The kind you can spot a mile away. Trying to act like they're from the 'hood but wearing designer jeans and smelling like baby food and hair gel."

"No names?"

"I've never seen them before. But they're all asking the same questions." Fred's black eyes snapped with interest as he sent Allie an appraising glance. "Apparently Special Agent Joseph Barnes's dead wife isn't dead."

Allie's fingers dug into the flesh of Mitch's arm.

He clamped his jaw. He liked Fred, and Fred had been a good contact when he'd worked undercover, but he wasn't going to endanger Allie's life by talking to him or anyone else about her.

He hung an arm around her neck and pulled her close for a quick kiss on her forehead. He spoke softly, as if he didn't think Fred could hear. "Don't worry about it, sweetheart. I don't even know who he's talking about."

Allie strained slightly against his embrace. "Yeah, right," she drawled.

Mitch covered his surprise with a short laugh, gave her a quick peck on her cheek and then turned back to Fred. "What about Bongiovi's goons? What do they want?"

Fred glanced at Allie and then back at Mitch, his dark eyes unreadable. "You know there's been talk for years that Bongiovi's untouchable. That he killed that deputy assistant director in return for protection."

Allie started at the mention of her father's murder. Mitch pulled her a little closer, and leaned down to whisper in her ear. "Hang in there. This is important."

She nodded and swallowed hard.

"Sure." Mitch knew the stories. Bongiovi had risen to power in the months following Deputy Assistant Director Harry MacNeal's execution-style murder. There had always been rumors that Bongiovi had been involved in the murder and that, in recent years, he'd been receiving protection from someone high up in the government. "That's just talk. Nobody's ever been able to figure out whose pocket he's in."

"Well, whoever it is wants you and Barnes's widow real bad."

"Maybe Bongiovi's working alone."

"No way. Man's got the Midas touch. DeSanto had a hold on this town ten years ago. Now DeSanto can't blow his nose without getting pulled in for littering. Bongiovi's getting help from somewhere." Fred stopped and straightened as a young man peered in through the dirty front window, then gave up and walked away. Fred turned his attention back to Mitch. "Lately though, I hear he's been pulling back."

"Pulling back?"

Fred nodded. "He's got kids. A pretty wife. And he's got a cousin who's becoming known in the community. Could be the cousin's being groomed to take over."

Aware of the time slipping away, Mitch filed that information in his brain and zeroed in on his purpose for looking up Fred. "Ever hear from Hangout?"

Fred spread his large, long-fingered hands. "I happened to run into him yesterday. He's not interested in going back inside."

"If he's got what I need, he won't have to. Where is this place you mentioned, where he eats?"

"Moc's? It's on Sixteenth. Walk straight on over. You can't miss it." Fred looked at the Rolex on his wrist. Mitch recognized it. "He could be there right about now."

"Okay, Fred. Thanks."

As Mitch turned to leave, Allie tugged on his arm. She leaned up and whispered in his ear, her breath tantalizingly warm against his earlobe. "Shoes for Baby, please."

Mitch had to bite his cheek to keep from laughing. Allie surprised him more every day. She was a pretty good actress. Impressive, after what she'd just heard. Mitch knew Allie was upset over the talk of her father's murder. "Hey, Fred."

The tall black man was about to disappear through the interior door. He stopped.

"Baby here needs some shoes better suited to walking."

Fred looked at Allie's legs and feet. "Shame to cover up those pretty toes."

Anger flared inside Mitch, shocking him with its intensity. Was he feeling jealous? He'd never felt like this about a woman. Controlling himself with difficulty, he settled for stepping closer to and slightly in front of Allie, sending a signal to the other man that he knew he would understand. A signal of ownership.

Allie forced herself to continue to play her part. Fred's mention of her father's murder had shaken her. Was he saying Bongiovi had killed her father? Even worse, was he saying that someone in the government had engineered it?

Dying to ask Mitch but knowing she couldn't until they were alone, she cocked a hip. Her ankle in the impossibly high shoes nearly gave way. She caught herself against the wall. "And a jacket, too," she whined, sending Mitch a pouty look. "Please?"

A couple of minutes later, her feet encased in worn tennis shoes and a hooded sweat jacket tied around her waist, Allie breathed a huge sigh of relief as she hurried to keep up with Mitch's longer stride. Her feet and legs still ached from the high heels, but at least every step wasn't agony. "I have long legs, but you're tough to keep up with," she called to him.

He slowed.

She slipped her hand through the crook of his arm again. It was easier to keep up when she hung on to him, and it made her feel safer. "If I'd had to walk one more step in those heels, you'd be carrying me back to our room."

"I can still take you back there. You don't need to go with me to find Hangout."

Allie stopped, hanging on to Mitch's arm, forcing him to stop, too. She looked up at him. Why couldn't he understand?

"Yes, I do, Mitch. I need to. Maybe if I see Hangout, hear him talk, it will jog my memory."

"I don't like it." He pulled her close as a group of swaggering kids walked by. Cradled by his arms, she thought about his reaction to Fred's comment about her toes. She hadn't missed his swift, protective response. Fred's comment was just a harmless flirtation, like hundreds of people make to each other every day. But Mitch had moved in like a protective alpha wolf or lion, staking his claim.

To Allie, it had been a highly charged, sexy display of masculine dominance. She shivered in secret pleasure. It had made her feel feminine, powerful, in a way she'd never experienced. What did it say about her that in the midst of a struggle for her life, she'd reacted so strongly, so sexually, to the man who held her safety in his hands?

What did his actions say about him? She glanced sidelong at him. He'd never been anything but a perfect gentleman and his respect and deep affection for Joe had been obvious. But did his help represent more than just duty?

Once the kids passed, he let go, his jaw muscle working. "Out here, you're in danger. People are looking for us. You heard what Fred said. Not just the police, not just the Bureau. But the major crime lord in the area, too."

"What was Fred talking about? Was he saying Bongiovi killed my father?"

"As long as I've been in the Bureau, there have been rumors that Bongiovi killed your father. Either working alone or for someone in the government, maybe even in the Bureau, who was looking to move up. Everybody's got a theory."

"I know, I've read all the news articles. What's yours?"

He shrugged. "I don't see how Bongiovi would have benefited from killing your father. Unless your father was giving protection to DeSanto—" he held up a hand before Allie could protest "—which we know he wasn't."

"So who do you think killed him?"

"One theory is that Bongiovi proved his ruthlessness and bravery by performing that hit on your father, and afterward it was a snap to take over power from DeSanto."

"Why didn't somebody arrest him?"

"He was questioned, but he had an airtight alibi for the time of the murder. Just like he was questioned after Joe's murder. His alibi for that night was even more airtight. He was the guest of honor at a benefit dinner. He sat at the head table the whole evening." He shot her a narrow look. "Now as I was saying, why don't I take you back to the room, then I'll go talk to Hangout."

"As *I* was saying, I feel safer with you than alone."

Mitch frowned. "That'll be small comfort to either of us if I let you get shot." He circled her waist with his hand and headed toward Sixteenth Street.

Hesitantly, Allie slipped her hand under his coat and around his lean waist, her fingers brushing the leather of his holster.

When they reached Sixteenth Street, Mitch pulled Allie a little closer and nodded. "There's the place."

Moe's was a little hole-in-the-wall place. An old, flickering neon sign said *M e 's*. The *O* was dark. Mitch shoved open an ancient glass door with corroded chrome handles and walked inside ahead of Allie.

She clung to his arm and tried to look bored and

tired. She was afraid she looked more hungry than anything else though. The fragrance of hot fresh coffee mingled with the mouth-watering smell of bacon frying and bread baking to send pangs of hunger through her belly.

She sat down at the counter while Mitch stuck a toothpick in his mouth and surveyed the skinny shotgun room.

He sat down beside her. "He's not here."

"Well, as long as we are—" she whispered, holding out a menu to him.

He smiled indulgently and nodded. "I'm hungry, too," he said, his fingers brushing hers as he took the menu.

THEY STAYED at Moe's for a couple of hours, but Hangout never showed. Mitch wondered if Fred had tipped him off and scared him away. Not wanting to alert Hangout or call attention to himself or Allie, Mitch didn't ask about him. Finally, he stood and threw some bills on the counter.

"We'd better get back. I'll come back over here later. See if he shows up for dinner."

"I'll come with you. We can see what the special is."

Mitch heard the hesitant hope in Allie's voice. He, too, was pleasantly full from a big, satisfying breakfast, the first real meal they'd had. "We'll see," he said.

"Great." Allie stood and headed toward the door. "When my father said that, it always meant no."

"Your father must have been a very frustrated man, then. Because in my experience, you never take no for an answer." He pushed open the door for her.

Allie grinned at him as she passed, and he'd have

sworn she put an extra swing in her walk just for him. He couldn't help watching the back of her little black skirt, even as he lectured himself about staying focused.

She was probably just feeling the surprisingly euphoric effects of fresh coffee and a hot meal. Both of them deserved a few minutes respite from the nonstop tension of the past three days.

As they walked back toward the rooming house, Allie pulled on the zippered sweatshirt Fred had given her and tugged on the bottom of her skirt.

With the baseball cap, the miniskirt, tennis shoes and the sweatshirt hiding the red bra that showed like a beacon through her T-shirt, Allie looked like a kid. Mitch could imagine her, gangly and tomboyish, playing ball.

Mitch walked a few steps behind her, admiring her shapely figure and long gorgeous legs as he maintained a careful watch to be sure they weren't being followed.

After a few blocks, she slowed down.

"Had enough?" she asked saucily.

His eyes followed a dark sedan until it turned a corner and disappeared. "Enough what?"

"Of watching me walk." She grinned at him again.

"I wasn't watching you. I was watching that car."

"Yeah, right." She pushed the bill of her baseball cap up. "Mitch?"

He slid his arm around her waist and grimaced as his fingers touched the swell of her hip. He liked to keep her close so he could shield her if anything happened, and so their conversations wouldn't be overheard. But he had to be more careful. Touching her was becoming a habit that would be hard to break.

"Did Joe ever talk to you about Hangout?" she asked.

"No. Nobody talks much about their informants. Informants are a special class of people. They're playing both sides, and they don't really trust either side."

"Just like neither side can trust them."

He nodded. "Right. So it becomes a balancing act. You take what they tell you and you evaluate it, and try to judge what's reliable and what's not. If too much turns out to be unreliable, then you find another informant."

"And I guess nobody knows whether Hangout was reliable or not." A strand of dark red hair fell out from under her baseball cap. She twisted it and stuffed it back up under the edge of the cap. "Now that Joe's gone."

She blinked and Mitch saw a dewy brightness in her eyes. She still missed her husband.

"What Hangout told the police after I identified him wasn't any help, and I doubt it was because of his loyalty to Joe."

Allie tilted her head to look at him from under the cap's brim. "So he was protecting the other side, whoever that was."

Mitch headed toward the grubby front doors of Hayes Rooms half a block ahead. Just as he was about to step into the street, two men pushed their way inside.

Allie was talking. "Do you think—"

"Shh." Mitch jerked her against him and put his hand over her mouth.

"Wha—"

He pulled them into an alley. "Quiet," he whispered. "I saw something."

He leaned out and took a quick glance down the street. Then he pushed her against the wall and flattened himself next to her, his left arm pressed protectively against her diaphragm.

"I just saw two guys dressed in black go into Hayes Rooms." He looked at her. "It could be nothing."

She nodded, then glanced beyond him at the other side of the street and gasped. "Mitch, look."

Two police cars raced past and squealed to a stop in front of the rooming house.

"What the hell?" he muttered as he watched the uniformed cops draw their guns and enter behind the other men. He couldn't tell from his vantage point whether the cops knew the other men were inside, but they obviously were after something.

A fugitive FBI agent and a protected witness maybe?

He glanced down the far end of the alley. He didn't know where it led, except that it was away from the excitement.

"Come on. It looks like they found us again."

Allie ran, with Mitch behind her, his hand pressed against the small of her back. At a juncture of alleys, he pulled her to the left.

"This way."

"Where are we going?" she puffed, glancing back toward him.

"Away from there. Some place where we can hide while I find out what that was all about."

Allie almost stumbled over the foot of a someone leaning against a Dumpster. She caught herself in time, and stopped to catch her balance and her breath.

The person she'd stumbled over was all bundled up, odd in the May heat. He or she was totally swathed in black, from a misshapen hat to a ragged scarf and coat. Nothing was visible but the eyes.

Allie's heart stopped dead in her chest.

"Allie?"

Hello, Allie.

She couldn't move, couldn't breathe, couldn't take her eyes off the ragged black scarf, the turned up collar, the hat.

Terror blasted her like an icy January wind.

Someone called her name again and pulled on her hand, but that wasn't real. Reality was inside her head, in front of her eyes, putting substance to the memories her brain had shielded her from all these months.

She wanted to scream. Needed to.

"Allie!"

Mitch.

His face in front of her eyes and his warm, insistent hands became her reality. She lunged toward him, reaching for the promise of his protection, toward the life that pulsed so strongly in him.

He wrapped her in his arms and, without question, pulled her on down the alley, away from her nightmare.

She clung to Mitch, but she couldn't resist a glance backward. The figure raised its head until Allie could see its face. A hook nose shaded a mouth filled with broken, yellowed teeth. He was just a scruffy homeless person, surrounded by garbage.

Mitch pushed Allie through a dark wood door. After the bright sunlight outside, Allie couldn't see anything, so she let Mitch guide her.

She felt as limp as a rag doll as Mitch led her to the back of the room. As her eyes became adjusted to the dimness, she saw small tables and chairs, a long wooden bar and rows of booths. He sat her down in a booth and slid in beside her.

Near the entrance, a television mounted above the bar blared some sports rehash from the night before.

She stared at it, clasping her hands together with the idea that if she held on to herself, she could keep from flying apart. She couldn't make out a word of what the announcer was saying.

Mitch touched her face, forcing her to look at him. "What happened back there?"

Shaking, Allie squeezed her hands tighter and hunched her shoulders. She resisted his questioning fingers. Closing her eyes, she found herself back there—in the hallway of her Georgetown home, reaching for the doorknob.

"Allie, look at me." Mitch's hard fingers wrapped gently but firmly around her jaw and turned her head to face him.

She obliged, trying to focus on his face, but all she could see was the darkness on the other side of the carved mahogany and beveled glass door of her Georgetown home.

"There was a shadow, nothing but dark."

"Where? Back there by the Dumpster?"

She shook her head, never taking her eyes off his. "When I opened the door." Her pulse drummed in her temples and she could hardly breathe. The flash of memory had gone by so fast. It had sheared through her like a bullet.

Now, trying to remember it was like watching a horrible tragedy in slow-motion video. She knew what was coming, but she couldn't stop it, she couldn't make it go any faster, and she couldn't change what was going to happen.

"Allie?"

Mitch was here. She couldn't change what she'd remembered, but he'd be there with her.

"You opened the door," he prompted.

"The shadow moved closer and I saw it was a man. All wrapped in black like—" Her breath caught on a sob.

Mitch put out his hand and she grabbed it, her fingers cold and clumsy. His pulsed with warmth, life, safety.

"Like the guy you ran into back there." His voice was sure.

She nodded, drawing strength from his steady hand, his calm demeanor. "You saw him?"

He nodded and a shaky little laugh escaped her throat. "I wasn't sure if—if he was real."

"I saw him." Concern etched the tiny lines around Mitch's eyes, and scored the corners of his mouth. "All bundled up like it was January."

January. Allie shivered. January fifteenth. The day Joe had died.

He pushed a fallen curl behind her ear. "What happened next?"

She shivered. "He moved like a shadow. I felt—something—a breath of fresh air? No, that doesn't make sense. It must have been the wind."

"Did you see his face?"

She shook her head.

"His eyes? Anything?"

"The shadow went around me and when I turned, it was moving toward Joe. Joe said something—and then—light flashed. Oh!" she gasped, expecting to hear the crack of gunfire.

A tear spilled over and rolled down her cheek. "The light was the gun firing, wasn't it?"

Mitch wiped her tear away with his thumb. "Allie, why did you let him in?"

The night, the cold, the black menacing shape tried to pull her back in, to become her reality again. She shook her head stiffly and tightened her grip on Mitch's hand. He leaned in slightly, as if to hold her here, in the present.

She stared beyond him. Why had she let the man in? "I—had to."

Mitch's blue eyes snapped with interest. "You had to—why? Did he hold a gun on you? Threaten you?"

"No." She shook her head, trying to sort out her odd feelings. She recalled feeling apprehensive but powerless. There was nothing else she could do but let him in.

"It was just that he was so big. *So powerful.*"

Mitch looked thoughtful. "Powerful. What did Joe say? How did he react when he saw the man?"

"I don't know." She let go of Mitch's hands and pressed her fists against the side of her head. Frustration choked her. "What is the matter with my brain? I knew the man. I let him in. Why can't I remember?"

"This is good. Your memories are starting to come back."

Allie closed her eyes, and the vision was clearer. She saw her newly decorated hallway, with its subtle recessed lighting, the Victorian oak gossip bench that held the hall phone, the double mahogany carved door. She heard the light click of her shoes on the Italian marble floor. She felt the cool brass doorknob under her fingers.

"No," she whispered, putting her hands over her eyes. "I don't want to—" she mouthed soundlessly, knowing it didn't matter what she wanted. She had to.

A deep, terrible shudder wracked her body when she

imagined standing there, where her blood and her husband's had spilled.

She didn't want to remember. As hard as it had been to accept that she and Joe had been shot in their home, she'd only known what had happened from police reports, depositions and a few photographs. Her brain had protected her from the pain and horror of what she'd seen.

But the price was high. Too high. She would never be safe, never be free of fear until she remembered everything about what had happened that night.

She fisted her hands on the tabletop. "I've got to go back there."

Mitch jerked. "What? Back to your house? No."

Mitch saw Allie's confusion at his abrupt response. He wondered what she'd say if he told her she wasn't the only one surprised at his vehemence.

His first instinct upon hearing her words was to grab her and shield her. She should never have to enter the place where she'd almost died.

He realized he wasn't sure he could face standing where he'd seen the dead body of his friend, where he'd knelt in Allie's blood and touched her matted hair, so afraid she would die.

"Do you know who bought it? I'm sure they'd agree to let me in."

"It's still on the market."

Allie frowned. "But I got money for it."

He nodded. "From the government. They gave you what the house was worth. Now they have it on the market. You're supposed to be dead, remember?"

She flinched, and he wanted to bite his tongue. But she straightened, not ready to give up.

"If it's empty, all the better."

He started to speak, but she went on.

"Mitch, it would work. If I stood there, if I opened the door, maybe it would trigger the memories and I could see his face."

"It's too dangerous," he said shortly, knowing that explanation wouldn't satisfy her.

"Why? We're in danger now. We don't even know who is after us. If I could remember, at least we'd know who we were running from." She glared at him. "You're still trying to protect me. Could you stop it? I just want this nightmare to be over. Going back there makes perfect sense. Are you afraid I might remember who really killed Joe, and prove that you were wrong about him?"

Pain lanced through Mitch's chest. She was upset, frightened. And he was the closest thing for her to lash out at. He knew that. But it didn't stop the stinging regret that he couldn't give her the one thing she'd asked for from the beginning—his unwavering belief in Joe's innocence.

He took her hands in his. "Allie, listen to me. I know you think I'm your enemy. I'm not."

His thumbs caressed her whitened knuckles. "I loved Joe. He taught me things my own father never did. The meaning of respect. The importance of integrity, of being true to myself." He blinked away a suspicious brightness in his eyes. "I miss him."

"I know. I do, too." She bit her lip. "But what if the man we miss is not the real Joe? What if we didn't know him at all?" A deep shudder racked her.

Through lips numb with fear and grief, Allie said the words she'd never had the courage to say. "I don't want to remember that Joe was guilty."

The admission sent tears spilling over her eyelids.

Mitch cupped her cheek in his hand and she pressed her face against his palm. She loved the gentle touch of those long sturdy hands that she knew were so strong. When he leaned closer, her eyes drifted shut, and she expected a kiss on her forehead.

But his lips brushed against hers. Pure desire flowed through her as she lifted her head to meet his kiss. An involuntary moan escaped her throat and his hand tightened, pulling her closer. For an endless moment, Allie let herself be taken over by the erotic pleasure of Mitch's mouth and tongue moving on hers. Nothing had ever made her feel so alive. No one had ever evoked the pure sexual response in her that he did with just the touch of his mouth.

Within seconds, both of them were breathless. Mitch pulled back slightly, to press his forehead against hers.

"I'm sorry. It's just—"

"Mitch, don't. Don't keep apologizing. We're both adults," Allie said wryly. "We have a connection."

He shook his head. "That's no excuse. You're in a vulnerable position. I'm supposed to be—"

She put her fingers against his lips. "If you say protecting me, I will walk out of here and you can just try and keep up with me."

Mitch thought wryly that keeping up with her was what he'd been trying to do since she'd called him from that phone booth. He opened his mouth to say so, but Allie's attention was no longer on him.

She grabbed his arm. "Mitch, listen."

She was looking at the television at the front of the bar. As he shifted his attention the droning voice from the set turned into words. Someone on the news was talking about Hayes Rooms.

...nor the police would comment on the reason for

the raid. It has been rumored that an FBI special agent and a witness in a major murder case involving another FBI agent are missing. It's not known at this time whether this incident is related to their disappearance. We will bring you more live coverage as it happens.

"Well, that explains the police," he said. "Come on. I don't think they'll be flashing any pictures of us on the screen, but we should get out of here."

As the after-work regulars crowded into the bar, Mitch and Allie slipped out.

Chapter Seven

Jack O'Hara glanced at his cell phone and saw Decker's number. By the time he got the phone to his ear, Decker was already talking.

"—the hell's going on?"

"The question is, where are you?" Jack pointed the remote control at the television in Decker's office to turn down the sound.

"Headed toward a little dive called Moe's."

Jack raised his brows. That was more information than Decker had revealed so far about his whereabouts. "I take it you caught the evening news?"

"Jack—"

"There was a slight disturbance at a little place called Hayes Rooms about twenty minutes ago. Seems a couple of unsavory characters headed straight for Room 2B. They kicked in the door and tore up the place. Wouldn't say what they were looking for."

Decker was silent.

"Then, less than five minutes after that, two of D.C.'s finest popped in, asking questions about a couple—tall white male, mid to late thirties, graying at the temples, female slender and leggy, with dark red hair."

"I notice the media had even more than that."

Jack nodded. "Yeah. Somebody tipped them off that you and Allie are missing. No names yet, although I'm sure it's just a matter of time. Conover is livid that the media knows the Bureau's involved. He's got no choice now. He has to do something."

"You said the guys weren't talking. Does that mean they were picked up?"

"Yep. Charged with vandalism. They're probably making bail as we speak. Just how many people did you give your location to? Were you planning an open house?"

"Nobody but Withers. And you're the only one who has this number."

"You don't think Allison—"

"No. I don't," Mitch broke in.

Jack heard a note in his friend's voice he'd never heard before. Jack's already tense frown deepened. So that's what this was all about. Decker was falling for Joe Barnes's wife. Having gone through that awful and blissful transformation from dedicated loner to head over heels in love himself recently, Jack knew the signs. This could be a problem.

Jack had been bemused by his friend's actions. Mitch Decker would go to the mat for any member of his team. He would take a bullet before he'd put any of them in unnecessary jeopardy. His disappearance and his refusal to tell anyone, even Jack, his location was so unlike him that Jack had begun to worry about his sanity.

But if it was love, well—then he was definitely worried about Decker's sanity. Although he'd have thought his controlled, careful boss would be the last person to throw it all away for a woman.

Jack made one more effort to get Mitch to see reason.

"Look, Boss, what if we put Allison in one of the police safe houses and let Storm guard her? Then even if someone knew where she was, they wouldn't be able to get to her." Jack knew there were holes in his logic, but maybe Decker would catch on and realize he couldn't do it all alone.

"Come on, Ice Man. They blew up her apartment. I can't afford to have anyone know her whereabouts."

"Well, someone does know. And whoever that someone is told the police." Jack pushed his fingers through his hair. "It's got to be Withers. You still trust him?"

"He saved my butt once. He's never let me down before. But no. I can't afford to trust anyone completely."

"If he's clean he should have already contacted you. Although I suppose he could be busy on a case. I think we need to question him. I'll have him picked up. I can work it so he thinks it's about a new location for you two."

"Anything else?" Decker asked.

"We got a hit on the prints from your office, and they were fresh, laid down within the last forty-eight hours. Still plenty of oils on them. Nothing on the phone, but a couple of nice partials off the doorknob. The partials were a match for a small-timer with a rap sheet for B and E. He doesn't remember being anywhere near the D.C. field office."

"He'd have had to have a pass to get into the building."

"Yep. We're looking into that now."

"Any chance he'll give it up?"

"Hard to say. Nat's running his telephone records and

his credit cards and bank accounts on the computer. Maybe we'll find something we can use for leverage."

Decker didn't speak for several seconds.

"Don't guess it would do any good to ask you what your next move is." Jack knew better.

"Nope."

Mitch had a long-standing reputation for playing his cards close to his chest, but Jack had never seen him like this. He only knew Allison Barnes from a few official functions with her husband, the Division of Unsolved Mysteries's previous boss. And he knew she was the daughter of Harry MacNeal, whose unsolved murder had rocked the foundations of the Bureau. He'd been impressed with her. He just hoped she didn't break Decker's heart.

"So what do you think, Jack? About the B and E guy?"

Jack sighed and turned off the television. The brief excitement at Hayes Rooms was over.

"You gotta love a stupid crook. Used gloves on the phone but not on the door. He removed the bug all right, which leads me to believe it was government issue. The question is, who got him in?"

"Someone who has access to the Bureau."

"That's the only conclusion that fits the facts."

"Let me know what Nat turns up."

"Sure thing. Oh." Jack glanced at his notebook. "I checked on Seacrest."

"Yeah?"

"He's still in prison, but he's got a parole hearing coming up. He's been meeting with his lawyer a lot. And guess who his lawyer is? A niece of Carmine Bongiovi's wife."

"I thought Seacrest had been in bed with DeSanto."

"Yeah. He was a hired gun. Didn't take him any time to switch allegiances."

"So we're back to Bongiovi."

"Looks like it."

"But Allie's never met Bongiovi, and she knew the killer."

"Yeah. Well here's another surprise. The license plate on that car that sideswiped you at the gas station? There's a restaurant near downtown, an Italian place. The owner's car has similar plates. He claims the car was stolen. This owner—he's connected to our favorite person—Bongiovi. Some second cousin by marriage or something."

"Damn."

"Yeah. So Decker? Are you coming in?"

"Not until I'm sure Allie's safe."

"Conover's on the warpath."

"He's not harassing the team, is he?"

"Nah. Just me."

Decker cut the connection. Jack stared at his cell phone for a few seconds, then deleted the number from its memory. Decker was covering all his bases. It was interesting that things kept pointing back to Bongiovi, but Jack had to agree with Decker's first assessment. The only conclusion that fit all the facts was that someone close to the Bureau was involved in the attempts on Allison Barnes's life. But who? And how high up did it go?

BY THE TIME Frank Conover left his emergency meeting with the assistant director for criminal investigations at the AD's house, he could have killed Mitchell Decker with his bare hands.

He'd just spent a half hour assuring the assistant director that no one knew one of his special agents in charge was AWOL, right before an aide came in to let the AD know about the television story. He'd promised the AD that it was only a matter of time before Decker was found and brought in. He'd also taken pains to explain to the AD that Decker was obviously distraught over the recent sudden death of his father.

Conover unbuttoned his suit jacket and got into his Lincoln Town Car. He called his special assistant on his cell phone.

"Sherbourne, how in the hell did the press get the information about one of our special agents being in the wind?"

"Obviously, someone thought it would be helpful if everyone knew."

"Obviously, we'd better find Decker before *someone else* does." Conover adjusted his cuff and checked his cuff links to be sure the double pearls were lined up correctly.

"We're making progress, sir. Unfortunately, we missed him at Hayes Rooms. The police on the scene reported that it looked like they'd been gone for a couple of hours, so they may have gotten a tip."

"Well, I'm in hot water with my boss, and you know how important it is to me to wrap up Special Agent Barnes's murder case."

"Right, sir. I'm on it. I expect to be talking to our contact shortly."

"Keep me posted. Next time I hear from the assistant director, I want it to be about my promotion."

"Right. Oh, by the way sir, it seems a small-time hood has resurfaced."

Conover sighed. "Yeah? Who?"

"Hangout Hooper."

"That little pip-squeak who was ratting to Barnes? What's he up to?"

"Not sure, sir. He could be working for Bongiovi again."

"Well, it would be good to keep an eye on him." Conover turned off the phone and headed for his office. He didn't have time to deal with small-time crooks. His people could take care of that.

He was still stinging from the dressing-down he'd gotten from his boss. One way or another, Decker would pay for embarrassing him before his assistant director.

As MITCH and Allie stepped into the crowded shotgun diner, Mitch spotted Hangout Hooper in a booth in the back, shoveling French fries into his mouth as if he were about to have his plate stolen. There was no mistaking that squirrelly face and the big-knuckled hands that seemed to belong to a much larger man.

They sat at the counter and Allie grabbed a menu. Mitch nodded at the gum-chewing waitress who greeted them with a raised coffeepot. She poured them each a cup.

Mitch kept an eye on Hangout, gauging the length of time before the little snitch would be done with his meal. At the rate he gnawed on his burger and slurped coffee, he'd be ready for his ticket in about five minutes. For a small man, he had a big appetite.

Mitch wrapped his hand around his mug, ignoring the handle, and nudged Allie. "There he is, last booth. Recognize him?"

Allie leaned forward and looked around Mitch. "No. Not at all."

"Let's see if he recognizes you. Keep your weapon

instantly available." Mitch surreptitiously checked his gun and sauntered down the single line of booths to the last one, with Allie right behind him. He let Allie in and slid in beside her, stretching his left arm across the back of the booth. He knew Hooper could see the edge of his shoulder holster.

"Harold Hooper, as I live and breathe." Mitch watched Hangout closely, but as soon as Hangout assessed them and put them in the *no immediate threat to life and limb* category, he went back to his food. Mitch figured that, like the runt dog in a litter, Hangout never missed an opportunity to eat.

He finished his last French fry and held up his cup, gesturing to the waitress.

"'On't go by Harold," he mumbled, chewing.

"You will soon, back in the joint."

The little man's head jerked up. "What for? Who the hell *are* you?"

When the waitress appeared with the coffeepot, Hangout held up his cup with a grimy hand. As soon as she was finished pouring, he downed a big swallow of the scalding hot stuff, then licked his lips.

"Get you two anything?" she asked, popping her gum.

Before Mitch could even ask, Allie spoke up. "Give me a turkey on wheat with mayonnaise and a side salad."

"You got it, hon."

"I'll take the steak sandwich with slaw. Bring us a box, in case we have to run, and go ahead and give me the tab."

When the waitress left, Mitch turned his attention back to Hangout, who hadn't taken his eyes off him. "I hear you're violating parole. All I have to do is make a phone call, and you'll be right back inside."

Hangout's muddy brown eyes glinted with fear for an instant. Then he eyed Allie with suspicion. "I ain't done nothing," he whined. "Just a little something to keep body and soul together. Nothing for you boys to get excited about. Leave me alone. Giving me indigestion."

Mitch let Hangout stew until the waitress came back with their orders. He gave her a twenty, waved away the change and told her they wouldn't be needing anything else.

"I want a piece of apple pie," Hangout said.

Mitch shook his head at the waitress.

Mitch stuffed his wallet into the tight jeans, then draped his arm over the seat back again, feeling a need to shield Allie from what was about to come. "Later. You were Joe Barnes's contact."

"Whoa, whoa, whoa." Hangout showed his broad palms. "I know who you are. You were in court. Are you a cop? And who's she?"

Allie stiffened, and Mitch gave a quick prayer of thanks that her mouth was full of turkey sandwich. He was relatively sure she wouldn't say anything foolish, but she knew she was sitting across from a man who had likely been involved with her husband's murder, and Mitch could feel the anger and frustration radiating from her body like a fever.

"All you need to know is I need some information about Barnes, and I know for a fact that you were meeting with him."

Hangout finished his coffee and leaned forward. "No need to announce it to everybody. So what if I met with him a few times? I met a lot of people."

Mitch adjusted his coat so Hangout was certain to see

his weapon, then dropped his arm so it rested lightly against Allie's shoulders. "Did all of them end up dead right after they talked to you?"

Hangout's gaze went from the gun, to Allie and to Mitch's face. He looked a little queasy. "You're the one who followed me. You ID'd me."

"I need to know what you discussed."

"Aw, man, that's so long ago, I forgot."

"Did you forget you're on parole?"

Hangout's close-set eyes narrowed. "You can't prove anything."

Mitch leveled his gaze at Hangout. "Stop jerking me around, Harold. You know I can put you back in. You don't like it in there, do you? A little scrawny guy like you."

The little man's Adam's apple bobbed up and down. "Do we have to do this here?" He spoke in a stage whisper. "Anybody could be listening."

"We could go down to the police station."

"Naw, naw. All I meant was maybe we could take a quick walk." He looked over at Allie. "Alone."

"There's no way you're going anywhere without me," Allie said with her mouth full. She quickly wrapped up the rest of her sandwich and took a last drink of coffee.

Mitch knew better than to try and talk her into sitting in the diner while he and Hangout talked alone. He nodded and stood, a sense of dread weighing down his limbs. He didn't like exposing her.

Allie reached for his sandwich.

"Leave it," he said to her. "Let's go."

Hangout threw some bills on the table and headed outside, hurrying across the street to a narrow alley.

Mitch stopped Allie with a hand on her arm, but she shook it off. "Don't even try."

"Be ready for anything," Mitch said gruffly. "I mean *anything.*"

Allie saw and heard the gravity in his voice. She looked at her wrapped-up turkey sandwich with regret, then threw it away and slid her hand into her half-open purse. Her fingers curled around the cold metal of the SIG. The thought of actually using it made her stomach churn, but she knew she could if she had to.

She met Mitch's gaze with the calm assurance she knew he'd expect in one of his agents. "I'm ready."

His practiced eye assessed her, and he nodded.

She felt like she'd passed a test.

She followed Mitch across the street and into the alley right behind Hangout. Her impression of the man was that he could not have put together any kind of sophisticated plan alone. He had to be working for someone with a lot more power and a lot more intellect.

Hangout walked a few feet into the alley, looked down it to where it opened out onto the next street, and then turned back to them. "Now, where were we?"

Allie saw Mitch clench his fists and then consciously relax them. She knew how he felt. She wanted to jerk the little squirt up by his ear.

"Joe Barnes."

Hangout looked cornered. "Hey. I took a few messages was all."

"Messages from who—to who?"

Hangout's eyes darted from Mitch to Allie and back. "What's the deal here? And what's in it for me, man?"

"The 'deal' is none of your business. What's in it for

you? If you get hauled in, I vouch for you, but only if you tell me the whole truth."

"You're Feebs, aren't you?" he said, using the slang term for FBI agents. "Man, I heard you was looking for me."

Mitch didn't bother commenting. Allie tightened her grip on her gun.

"Look, man, I already gave all I knew up to the lawyers after the shooting went down."

Mitch propped his fists on his hips. "See? That's too bad. That means I've got to go find somebody who knows more than you told the lawyers. I need somebody who knows what Joe Barnes said that afternoon that got him killed."

Swallowing hard, Allie listened to the exchange with a peculiar unease. She felt exposed, body and soul. She was standing in the middle of an alley, listening to two men discussing the death of her husband.

"Come on, man. I swear." Now Hangout was pacing nervously, glancing up and down the alley. "I ain't got no idea how he got dead. I didn't have nothing to do with that." He patted his shirt pocket as if looking for a cigarette, then his pants, then his shirt again.

"I can't stay here. I gotta get out of here. Anybody sees me with you and I won't be worth dog food."

Suddenly, moving so quickly Allie had no time to react, Mitch grabbed the shorter man up by his collar.

"If you had nothing to do with it, what were you talking to Special Agent Barnes about? And why would anyone in the world care if they saw you with me?"

"I don't know, man. I just heard."

Mitch lifted him up off his feet. "I changed my mind. I won't put you back in the joint. I'll just beat your scrawny butt and leave you here for the rats." He aimed a fist at Hangout's pale face.

"No, wait. Wait!" Hangout squirmed. "You don't understand. I could be killed if I talk to you."

"You *will* go back to prison if you don't."

The little man's eyes bulged, showing white around the pupils. Allie watched Mitch with ever-increasing admiration. Was there nothing he couldn't do? He was hard as nails when necessary, but could change like a chameleon by just altering his stance. He wore his integrity like a badge. Yet she also knew the depth of his feelings. His grief over Joe's death and the tenderness and compassion that he kept hidden, she realized, were what drove him more than anything else, even his sense of justice.

Right now, she wouldn't want to be in Hangout's shoes, which were barely touching the ground.

His prominent Adam's apple bobbed up and down as he swallowed. "Okay. Okay," he choked out. "I'll tell you what I know, but it ain't much."

"Too bad for you if it's not enough." Mitch loosened his grip on Hangout's shirt without letting go. The little man rolled his eyes to the right, obviously considering making a break. But a subtle shift in Mitch's position had him trying to press himself back into the wall.

Allie could see the terror in his eyes and understood it. No one with anything to hide would want to be within fifty feet of Mitch Decker.

Hangout certainly didn't. He squirmed uselessly.

"Okay, okay," he squeaked, starting to reach for Mitch's hand on his shirt collar, but thinking better of it. "Barnes was doing some deals for Bongiovi."

Allie gasped audibly. "No," she whispered, her limbs suddenly slack with shock.

Hangout's beady gaze slid to hers, and she stiffened. She'd promised Mitch she could do this. She had to push her fears aside and act like a seasoned agent. Mitch was counting on her.

Mitch stood ominously still for an instant, then slammed Hangout's head back against the brick wall hard enough for Allie to hear the crack. "You're lying."

His vehemence was a little frightening, and more than a little thrilling. Maybe Mitch wasn't as certain as he seemed to be about Joe's guilt. Maybe he really was looking for the same truth that she was.

"Ow. No! I swear. Larry Wills was killed when Barnes sent him to frame a rival dealer for a drug deal of Bongiovi's that went bad."

The stark, damning words made Allie feel sick. She clutched her stomach and looked at Mitch, hoping to draw assurance from him that Hangout was still lying.

But Mitch's mouth had gone white at the corners and a muscle in his jaw ticced. "You're saying Barnes got Special Agent Wills killed? How come a little punk like you knows something like that?"

Hangout drew himself up. "I was Joe's CI. I brought him messages."

"From Bongiovi."

Hangout's gaze shifted. "I wasn't no messenger boy for Mr. Bongiovi. I drove for him."

Mitch raised a brow. "A driver could hear lots of things. See lots of people. Who'd you see, Hangout? What did you hear?"

Hangout shook his head. "Nobody. Nothing. I can't

say nothing else unless you get me a deal. Put me in protective custody. I tell you everything. Just don't let him kill me."

"Who, Harold? Don't let who kill you?"

Hangout's eyes got wide as saucers. "Call somebody. Get me to a safe place. Call now."

Mitch let go of the little man's shirt with a disgusted grunt. "Sorry, Hangout. That's not good enough. The last time you promised that, you held out on us. I guess you're just going to have to die out here." Mitch looked at Allie. "Let's go," he said. "This place stinks."

"No. Come on, man. You can't leave me here now."

"Then stop dancing around and give me what you've got. And it better be worth it."

Hangout's pale face took on a faint flush of color as he grinned. "Oh, it is. It's big. Bigger than you can imagine. We're talking major players here. You'll be giving me a medal."

Mitch sent him a sidelong glance filled with disgust. "I doubt that. But you just might survive. Now, what major players?"

Over Mitch's low threatening voice, Allie heard the crunch of shoes on pavement behind her. "Mitch," she called softly, but he'd already heard it.

"Down, Allie!" he shouted as he grabbed for Hangout and jerked him down next to the wall on the other side of the alley.

Allie pulled out her SIG and crouched back behind a foul-smelling bag of garbage. She felt the rush of adrenaline through her veins, pumping blood faster and faster, causing her to gasp for breath. The smell of rotting food and soured milk made acrid saliva pool in her mouth as her stomach clenched in protest.

Whoever had stepped into the alley wasn't moving. Allie glanced at Mitch. He was inching up the wall, at a disadvantage because the gun in his right hand was simultaneously pressed against the wall.

Hangout hid behind Mitch's bulk, sweat streaming down his skinny cheeks. The collar of his shirt was already wet. His eyes rolled. He was on the edge of hysteria. Allie was afraid he was going to do something stupid.

She heard another crunch and then a pop. Gunfire.

"Stay back," Mitch growled.

Hangout screeched and jumped up.

Mitch reached for him, but his fingers missed Hangout's shirt as the snitch turned his back and started running up the alley.

More shots rang out. Mitch returned fire, but Allie watched Hangout, not breathing, knowing what she was going to see but unable to tear her gaze away.

"Get down!" she shouted at him as gunfire peppered the walls beside him, sending chips of plaster and grout flying in little white puffs. More slugs stirred dust and dirt around his feet.

Hangout paid no attention to her.

Then he dropped.

Just like that. One second he was running, the next he was nothing but flesh and bone and blood.

Allie cried out involuntarily. Even from six feet away, she could see the hole in the back of Hangout's head and the blood staining the ground.

For an instant, her vision turned black. Had Joe dropped like that? Had she?

A pop sounded in her ear and something hit her cheek.

Chapter Eight

Allie's ear rang from the ricochet of the slug off the wall near her head and her cheek stung. She whirled to see Mitch crouched behind a stack of boxes, firing nonstop.

Down the alley, two men were advancing slowly, holding semiautomatic rifles, and firing at them.

She lifted the SIG, dismayed at how her hand shook. She gripped the gun in both hands, as she'd been taught, and aimed to kill.

Between her gunfire and Mitch's, they forced the two men to take cover back against the wall.

"How far to the end of the alley?" Mitch called softly.

She took another shot as she saw the guy on her left raise his gun. "About fifteen feet."

"Hangout?"

She realized Mitch hadn't taken his eyes off the advancing men.

"He's about halfway. Dead."

"I'll cover you. Run."

Allie looked over at him. He jerked his head backward.

"And go where?" she asked. "I'll stick here with you."

Her last words were cut off by gunfire. She ducked back.

"Run to Fred's. You can find his place, can't you?"

A shot plowed through the brick above Mitch's head. The two men advanced again.

Mitch stood and took a couple of careful shots. A cry told Allie he'd hit one. Allie aimed at the other man, who was drawing a bead on Mitch.

She fired.

Her shot missed, but it was close enough that the man jerked as he pulled his trigger.

Beside her, she heard Mitch's soft grunt. He was hit.

"No!" she shouted, firing again and again, afraid to take her eyes off her targets, and afraid to look at Mitch. What would she do if something happened to him?

She heard him move and then fire several shots in quick succession.

Relief washed over her, sending a trembling through her limbs. She gritted her teeth to try to stop her hands from shaking as she ejected her empty clip. She pulled her second one from her purse, slammed it into place and then began firing rapidly again.

Sirens filled the air. One of the men shouted. They fired off another round, straight down the alley, then turned and ran, one of them listing to the right and clutching his side. Allie heard the screech of tires and watched the men disappear around the corner.

The warning blasts of a police siren echoed through the narrow alley, and Allie heard brakes squealing and a crash.

Mitch made a pained sound as he rose. "Let's go."

"Are you okay? Were you hit?"

"Later." Mitch ignored Allie's panicked voice. He was worried about her, too. There was blood on her cheek, but there was no time to be concerned about small injuries. The police were too close, and Mitch knew if they got picked up now, before he'd uncovered the answers, he'd lose any chance of ensuring Allie's safety.

He grabbed her hand and, staying close to the wall, they ran past Hangout's dead body and turned left onto the next street.

Behind them Allie heard the faraway pounding of feet on the pavement. The police.

Mitch hailed a cab. The cabdriver took one look at them and turned his Off Duty sign on, but Mitch flashed his badge. "FBI," he shouted through the open window. "Let's go."

The man gave a pained sigh and nodded.

Mitch climbed into the back seat after Allie and leaned back carefully. A slug had grazed the top of his shoulder and he could feel blood oozing out to stick to his shirt. Thank God the leather of his holster had deflected the slug.

He gave the cabbie the address to Fred's place. "Faster the better."

Next to him, Allie was trembling. "God, I hate this," she said.

"I know. Hang in there, Allie. It's going to be all right."

"All right? We just saw a man killed. *You* were almost killed."

He put his hand over hers. "Shh. Not so loud."

She crossed her arms and turned her head away, but

not before he saw the tears that brightened her eyes. He hated it, too. He hated that everything he did put her in danger more. He hated that he couldn't get a straight answer about anything, that every time he thought he had a lead it turned into another dead end or another twist.

"Why don't you just turn this over to Conover, or to Elkins?"

"If I did that, the first thing that would happen is they'd separate us. You belong with the U.S. Marshal's program and that's where they'd send you. My hands would be tied by the Bureau. You came to me because you didn't trust the people who'd been assigned to protect you. I violated a dozen regulations when I met you that night."

As he talked, her body grew more and more rigid, until he thought she might crack.

"I'm sorry I got you involved," she said stiffly.

"Damn it, Allie. That's not what I'm saying. I'm thankful you trusted me. But think about it. As soon as we talked, someone knew. From the beginning, someone has known nearly every move we've made."

Allie's gaze met his.

"I don't know who to trust."

The cab pulled up in front of Fred's building. Mitch pulled crumpled bills from his coat pocket and counted out twice the fare.

He glanced up and down the street, then he and Allie entered Fred Scarbrough's crack house.

As always, Fred was there to greet them.

"If it ain't Mr. Dixon and his lady friend."

"Scarecrow. We need a room. Got one with a shower?"

Fred's sharp eyes took in Mitch's bloody shoulder

and Allie's scraped cheek. "I got one or two, but they's expensive."

"I'm good for it."

Fred pulled on his ear. He was putting on for someone. "Well, I reckon that's true. You need anything else?"

"Just towels and privacy."

The black man's teeth showed in a wide grin. "I can understand why. Come on, then."

Mitch put his right arm around Allie's waist as they walked down the dark hall and up the stairs. The place reeked of unwashed bodies and drugs. A couple of rooms didn't have doors, and Mitch squeezed Allie closer to him as they walked past kids passed out on cots, a grizzled old man moaning in a corner and a young woman staggering toward the end of the hall, where presumably she was looking for a bathroom.

At the other end of the hall, Fred unlocked a door. "This here's the penthouse," he said wryly. "If I'm full, I'll open it up for the bathroom, but generally I keep it for special customers. Y'all can have it tonight."

Mitch stepped in and surveyed the room quickly. It wasn't nearly as bad as he'd expected.

"Go on in, Allie. I'll be right there."

She looked at him suspiciously, but did as he said.

He turned to Fred. "Can we talk?"

"Sure. In my office."

"I'd rather do it here."

"Not in the hall." Fred slouched over. "Can we talk in front of her?"

Mitch didn't have much choice. He nodded and the two of them came into the room and Fred shut and locked the door behind them.

Allie was standing with her arms crossed, looking out the window. She barely acknowledged them.

"What did you tell Hangout?"

"Me? Nothing. I just said ole Dixon was looking for him. He acted like he didn't know who you were. But he did. I could tell."

"What do you really know about him?"

"He's in with Bongiovi, but he isn't as in as he thinks he is. Drove for Bongiovi for a while, but as scrawny as Hangout is, he's got a big mouth on him."

"Was."

"Was?" Fred's eyes widened. "He's dead?"

"Barely. Just a while ago."

Fred looked at Mitch's shoulder.

"I need to know who knew we were going to talk to him."

"They didn't get it from me, man, but I'm sure you know, walls have ears."

"What about Withers? You mentioned you'd heard he was asking about Barnes's wife."

Fred shook his head. "I know you worked with him, but my personal opinion? He'd sell his mother."

Mitch nodded, glancing at Allie, who still hadn't moved.

"Okay. Can we get towels?"

"They're in the bathroom."

Mitch raised his eyebrows.

"I *told* you this room was the 'penthouse,'" Fred reminded him.

"What about clothes? You got anything clean we could wear?"

"Yours are still here. I'll bring them."

"Thanks, Fred. I don't suppose you could scare up some bandages."

"Now you think it's a five-star hotel?"

Mitch gave him a wry grin.

"I'll see what I can find."

"Fred, if anyone—"

Fred held up his hands. "I deal on a cash basis. I don't know any of my clients' names." He smiled. "How do you think I've managed to stay out of trouble?" He gave Mitch a half salute and left.

Mitch locked the door and walked over to where Allie stood at the side of the window, looking down on the street.

"Are you afraid they followed us?" he asked, putting a hand on her shoulder.

She shrugged it off and stepped away, shaking her head. She glanced at his shoulder, without raising her eyes to meet his gaze. "Let me help you with your shoulder."

He shrugged and then winced when his holster scraped raw skin. "It's just a graze. Soap and water will do just fine. Fred's going to see if he has some bandages." He approached her carefully.

"What about your cheek?"

"What about it?"

"Some flying debris scratched your face. You've got blood on your cheek."

She touched the dried trickle of blood as if she'd just noticed the feel of it on her skin. She looked at her fingers then brushed at a couple of tiny flecks that clung to them.

He reached out his hand, but she averted her head. "I'm fine. How did they know we were meeting Hangout? We didn't even know if we'd find him."

"That's what's bothering me about this whole thing. I'll give Jack a call. See what he can glean. It's my guess someone was tailing *Hangout*. Maybe looking for us, maybe for another reason entirely."

"Who do you think had him killed?"

"My guess? Carmine Bongiovi. But Hangout bragged about driving for him. I don't think Bongiovi was the 'major player' that Hangout mentioned."

Allie pressed her lips together, her face white. "You want the shower?"

He shook his head. "No. I'll wait for Fred to bring the clothes. You go ahead. He'll be back before you're done."

Allie retreated into the bathroom and Mitch dialed Jack.

"Oh, hi, Holly." Jack's deep voice was hushed.

"Question."

"Yeah, I'm in the middle of what looks like a shootout right now. Whatcha need?"

"Was there ever a question that Joe framed Special Agent Wills?"

There was a few seconds of silence. "No. Let me call you back, okay?"

Mitch disconnected. Jack knew it was him on the phone. So Jack was in a position where he couldn't talk. Apparently he was in the alley across from Moe's where Hangout's body was.

How had the FBI gotten involved so soon in what could have easily been put down as a drug deal gone bad? And why was Jack in the middle of it?

Chapter Nine

Mitch heard Allie turn on the shower as he sat down on the edge of the bed to check his gun and reload the clip. He paused, listening to the changing sound of the water as Allie moved under the spray. The thought of her creamy skin, wet and slick with water and soap, sent his blood surging downward. He berated himself for having so little control over his emotions around her.

He gave the clip a final inspection and slapped it back into the gun with more force than necessary, just as a discreet knock sounded on the door.

His gun in his right hand, Mitch stepped over to the door. "Yeah?" he said gruffly.

"Y'all wanted some clothes." It was Fred, in his Scarecrow persona.

Hiding his gun hand behind the door, Mitch unlocked it and cracked it open.

"Here you go." Fred handed him a bundle in a plastic grocery bag.

"Thanks. If you hear anything—"

"You got it, dog."

Mitch nodded and closed the door. The shower cut off right about then, so he knocked lightly on the bathroom door. "Allie? Your clothes are here. I'm going to hand them in, okay?"

There was silence for a minute. "Okay," she said in a small voice and cracked the door open. Her small damp hand, pink with the heat of the shower, came around.

Mitch handed her the bag, averting his eyes. How could the mere sight of her hand make his body hard with desire? "Leave mine in there," he said gruffly.

She didn't answer, just closed the door.

Mitch was worried about her. She'd been quiet and pensive ever since the shootout. He could put it down to being targeted by semiautomatic weapons in an alley and watching a man murdered before her eyes. That was enough to frighten anyone. But as much as he knew that had affected her, there was something else on her mind.

Death had followed Allie throughout her life. From her mother's death to her father's murder and her husband's, and the attempts on her own life.

Through it all, she'd been strong. Today, she'd shot a man, and she'd watched a man die in front of her. Of course Hangout's death bothered her. But that wasn't what was weighing so heavily on her mind.

Mitch was certain he knew what she was so upset about. It was Hangout's damning statement about Joe's involvement in the killing of Agent Wills.

Mitch wasn't sure she could bear it if Joe were guilty.

When she came out of the bathroom in her butterfly T-shirt and discount store jeans with a towel around her hair, he could see the scratch on her cheek was raw. Mitch found himself almost overcome with the urge to kiss it, to hold her close and make her promises he couldn't keep.

He forced a smile to his lips. "Feeling better?"

"Yes, thank you," she said, but her shoulders drooped and she didn't answer his smile.

"I'm going to shower. The door is locked. If you hear anything, you come into the bathroom. Don't open the door to the room. Not for anyone."

"Okay."

Mitch assessed her for a second. "Allie, are you okay?"

She nodded stiffly. "Fine."

"I'll be right out."

She raised her gaze to his for an instant and gave a tiny nod. "I know."

Worried about her but not knowing what to do, Mitch went into the bathroom and carefully peeled the leather holster and shirt from his skin. The bleeding started again. He peered in the distorted mirror to assess the damage. As he'd thought, it was a flesh wound, but the furrow went deeper than he'd realized. He quickly showered, paying special attention to cleaning his shoulder, even though it hurt like hell.

After he dried off, he blotted the wound with some toilet tissue, using a square of tissue as a temporary bandage until the bleeding stopped.

"Wow, IT FEELS good to be clean," he said as he came into the bedroom, having pulled on slacks after his shower.

Allie's head angled toward him, but she didn't turn. She was by the window again, her back to the room. She had pulled the blinds, and the room was shadowy, lit only by the streetlights and a flickering sign advertising a bail bondsman across the street.

She'd taken the towel off her hair and combed through it, and it fell in damp wavy tendrils to her shoulders. She had her arms wrapped around herself, as if she were holding herself together by sheer force of will. The T-shirt stretched across her back and Mitch could see the outline of the red bra clearly.

"Allie?"

For a few seconds, she stood still; then, she turned around. Mitch saw the wet trails of tears on her cheeks, and the despair in her eyes.

"Allie, what is it?" He started toward her, but she pulled in her shoulders. He stopped. "Talk to me. Let me help."

She blinked and pulled herself out of her daze. Her gaze focused on his shoulder. "You're bleeding."

"It'll stop. It's just a flesh wound."

"There were bandages in that sack. I'll get them." She started around him.

He stopped her with a hand on her forearm. "Don't worry about my shoulder. Tell me what's wrong."

She looked down at his hand and then pulled free. "I'll get the bandages," she said in a strained voice.

When she came out of the bathroom, she was all business. She gently pulled the tissue away from the wound, wiped it with clean damp tissue she'd brought from the bathroom and then dried it.

All Fred had given them were some small bandage strips, so she used three of them over the furrow the bullet had cut into the top of his shoulder. Her fingers were gentle but sure. Mitch closed his eyes and gave himself up to her care. It was the first time in his adult life, he realized, that he'd ever allowed a woman to do anything for him. He'd always been the caregiver, the strong one. It was his nature.

But by the time Allie finished her gentle ministrations, Mitch was not thinking at all about his wound or about his unusual role of taker rather than giver of comfort.

She'd been his boss's wife, but she wasn't any longer. She thought he was her enemy, but he knew he wasn't. And even if he could never be anything other than the man she'd trusted when she was in danger, he could at least take what comfort he could glean from moments like this.

He closed his eyes and took a deep breath, pulling in the scent of her. His body reacted to her closeness. A heavy ache, exquisite in its torture, throbbed in his groin.

"Did I hurt you?" she asked, pulling her hands away.

"No," he whispered, his voice strangled with unleashed passion. "No—not at all."

Her gaze met his and for a brief instant, a longing so fierce and needy shone in her eyes that it almost undid him. But she turned away, leaving Mitch to wonder if the look had even been there at all, or if it was a part of his impossible dream.

He should have been grateful that she'd moved away, that her shapely perfect body was no longer within his grasp, tempting him, but he wasn't.

Another man might have acted on that brief look in her eyes, might have grabbed her by the waist and pulled her back to him. But Mitch was more worried about her state of mind than about his state of discomfort.

So he stood, gritted his teeth and stopped his erotic daydreams. He was her protector. He was the only thing standing between her and danger.

And right now, he needed to be her confidant. She was upset. He'd help her if he possibly could. Coming up behind her, he put his hands on her shoulders, which were so tight he was certain they must be cramping.

"Tell me what's wrong," he said softly in her ear.

He felt her muscles tighten even more. She was like a rubber band, drawn to the last millimeter of its endurance, ready to snap. He massaged her shoulders gently, caressingly, as he tried to soothe her distress.

"Hangout was lying. About Joe causing that agent's death." Her voice was brittle.

Mitch grimaced. "Joe did send Wills out."

"He sent agents out every day. Just like you do now. How does the fact that he sent him out prove anything? You promised to help me."

"Allie, I promised to help you find the truth."

"The truth is that Joe was murdered!" she cried, wrenching her shoulders out of his grasp and turning on him. "Why are you so ready to believe a two-bit dealer? You know what kind of man Joe was."

"I do. But Allie, something *was* going on with him."

Allie spread her hands, grief and helpless rage sitting on her heart like a weight. "You want to know what was going on with Joe? He spent part of every day of his life on my father's case. That's what. Do you know why? Because he knew how much it meant to me. And because it meant that much to him."

She lifted her chin and looked at the man she'd thought she could trust. "But you wouldn't know about that, would you? You hated your father, so you have no idea what it's like to love someone that much. Like Joe loved my dad. Like he loved you. Like I—"

She stopped, cupping her hands over her mouth to

stop her too-rapid breathing. She couldn't face what she'd almost said. Facing it would mean she'd have to live the rest of her life under the cloud of danger that had hovered over her whole life. The FBI. Danger that not even her love could banish.

"—like I loved them," she finally finished. "I guess it's true what they say. Mitch Decker's a Bureau machine, with an FBI badge for a heart." Her bitter words were another cloud hanging between them.

Mitch closed his eyes briefly.

She'd hurt him. Even though it pierced her to the core to know that he didn't believe in Joe, she hadn't meant to lash out so cruelly.

When he opened his eyes, sadness and determination shone from them. "I never hated my father. I hated what he did. I hated the way he lived his life on the edge of decency. The way he would do anything for a buck." He brushed his hand across the top of his head and down the back of his neck.

He looked beyond her, into a place Allie had never seen. He was looking into his past. "I tried all my life to love him. He was my father. But I couldn't respect him. I respected Joe."

He pulled his gaze back to her, his eyes lit from within with resolve. "I want to prove Joe is innocent. I want to solve his murder. I want to ensure that you—" he reached out and brushed a fingertip across the scratch on her cheek "—that you'll never have to be afraid again."

"Don't worry about me." She slid past him. "I can take care of myself. I've had lots of practice. Did you know that I was the one who found my father, lying in the driveway with a bullet through his skull? I called the

FBI and secured the scene until they got there." She wiped the old, haunting images from her mind and took a shaky breath.

"Do you know who was first on the scene, and who stayed beside me through everything? And who promised me he would find Harry MacNeal's killer or die trying—" She couldn't continue.

Mitch nodded gravely. "I know. It was Joe. He loved you."

She nodded. "That's why I married him. He was there when I needed him."

Looking at him, Allie realized Mitch had done the same thing. He had been there beside her. He'd promised her he'd help her find Joe's killer. He'd promised her the truth.

She wrapped her arms around herself. Could she accept the truth, whatever it was? She knew that Mitch would accept no less. "Why do you believe Hangout?"

Mitch dropped his hands. "I don't believe or disbelieve him," he said softly. "But what he said made sense. I have to try and follow up. Maybe there was something about Wills's case that the investigators missed."

Allie nodded. *Of course.* He would do the logical thing. He would cover all the bases. Damn it, she was tired of doing the logical thing.

"Just once, could you do the illogical thing? Just once could you let your heart decide, instead of your head?"

Mitch considered the irony of her resentful words. They were running from the scene of a crime, hiding from the FBI, because he'd followed his heart and broken all the rules he'd lived his life by. The rules he'd sworn never to break. The logical thing would have been to contact the Witness Security Program and turn her over to them.

"You think what we're doing here is logical? We're witnesses. We fled the scene of a murder. I should be back there, cooperating with the police. It's my fault Hangout was killed. I should be letting the U.S. Marshal's Service do their job, which is protecting you. Instead, I'm sneaking around, letting other people do the real work. I haven't acted logically since you called me."

As he talked Allie's stiff back relaxed and her face softened into a look of regret. "I've forced you to go against everything you believe in."

Mitch shrugged, and winced when the movement hurt his wounded shoulder. "Not everything. But I need time to think. Time to process the information. We didn't get much from Hangout, but I need to think about how it fits in with everything else."

Allie took a shaky breath. "Now you sound like Joe," she said sadly. "He'd hole up in his office for hours when he thought he'd found a lead on my father's murder."

As Mitch wiped his face, Allie grabbed his arm. "Mitch, what if Joe found out who killed my father, and he was murdered to stop him from telling?"

Mitch knew the Bureau's answer to that. He also knew how little comfort that answer would give to Harry MacNeal's daughter. "Your father's murder was labeled a mob hit. Right after your dad's death, Carmine Bongiovi rose to power over the DeSanto family."

"But no one ever did anything, and the case was never closed, right?"

"Yes, and since then, there's been an ongoing investigation of Bongiovi's activities."

Allie laughed, although her eyes glittered with tears. "An ongoing investigation? For eight years? Give me a break. All that means is that the FBI has sat back and watched Bongiovi, and done nothing. Joe was the only one who cared what happened to my dad. Admit it."

"Joe would have given anything to solve your father's murder." Mitch sighed, forcing himself back to business. "I'll ask Jack to reopen the case, get Baldwyn to search for any similarities."

Allie stiffened. "Right. You just do that. And in eight more years, maybe someone will get around to it."

She gave a shaky sigh. "What am I going to do if Joe really was working for Bongiovi? If he really did deliberately send Agent Wills to his death?"

"Allie, look at me." She resisted, but he kept his grip on her shoulders firm but gentle as he turned her around. Her eyes were wet, her lashes spiky with tears, looking like dark starbursts around her green eyes.

"Agent Wills died in the line of duty. There was an official investigation. He died nobly." He bent his head and put his fingers under her chin, making her look up at him. "I don't believe Joe knew Wills would be killed. And I think if Joe was working with Bongiovi, he must have had a good reason."

"I've been trying to make myself believe Joe was guilty, trying to come to terms with it, like you seem to have, but I just can't."

Allie gazed up at Mitch, her insides in such turmoil that she couldn't even begin to sort out her feelings. So much had happened in such a short time. "I'm really scared, Mitch."

She was, of a lot of things. She was afraid Mitch would die. Seeing his blood had reminded her that he was human. That his body, no matter how strong, was not invincible. He could be killed.

She'd already lost her father and her husband. And both times, the grief and pain were almost more than she could bear.

If Mitch died—

She looked up at him and saw in his eyes that he knew what she was thinking. She saw something else, too. A tender, sweet softness in his eyes. A loving look.

Somehow, it frightened her more than anything else she'd seen in his eyes.

He touched the scrape on her cheek. "Nothing's going to happen, Allie. I can keep you safe."

She shook her head, her heart squeezing in pain. "You can't promise that. I understand the dangers. My father and my husband both died because of the Bureau. I don't know if I can bear it if—" Her voice gave out.

She just needed comfort. Someone to hold her. For a few minutes, she needed someone strong to take some of the weight. And Mitch was so strong.

Without allowing herself to think about anything except how close they'd come to death there in the alley, she slipped her arms around his waist and pressed her head against his shoulder.

She felt him stiffen.

"Allie, this—"

"Shh. Don't go all 'professional protector' on me, please," she said brokenly. "I need someone to hold me. Could you take off the badge for a minute, and be more than just Joe's friend who's doing his duty for the poor widow?"

She tightened her arms around his bare waist and turned her face to breathe in the clean, soapy scent of him.

His hands gripped her shoulders and he pushed her away, his face grim. "You think you want me. You may even think there's something between us. But once all this is over, you aren't going to want to ever see me again."

"That's not—"

He put his fingers across her mouth. "You said it yourself. You never want to be associated with the FBI again. No one would blame you. I can take off the badge, Allie. I did the minute you asked me to help you. But badge or not, I can't change who I am."

Allie looked up at his harshly beautiful face. When she'd bandaged his shoulder, her fingers had felt the steel-hard muscles covered with skin as smooth as finely tanned leather. The bullet's cruel path carved into that perfect flesh had made her want to cry.

She'd forgotten everything for that instant, except him, and when she'd raised her gaze to his, her fingers holding the bandage, she'd seen her own yearning reflected in his eyes.

Now, he filled her vision. The late afternoon shadows made a planed sculpture of his body, all honed angles and sinuous, ropy muscles, like a Rodin sculpture in a shady corner of a museum.

And like the sculpture, he was motionless, unyielding. His expression was intentionally hard. He was fighting his feelings for her.

"My loyalty is with the Bureau. It means I'll do everything I can to find the truth. No matter what that truth is."

"I know what you're doing," she said softly. "You're protecting my virtue. You've appointed yourself master of my fate." She put her hands against his bare chest, where blood and breath coursed through him. His diaphragm expanded and contracted with his rapid breathing.

"Look at us, Mitch. How many times can we outrun them? I'm afraid. I've lost everything—twice. I may lose everything again. But right now, I want—" She looked down, a little bit embarrassed. "I need to feel something besides fear. I need to hold on to something real, something solid."

Hesitantly, bracing herself for a gentle rebuff, she moved a step closer to him. When his hands released their grip on her shoulders and slid around her back, she let out the breath she'd been holding.

Lifting her head, she read his surrender in his eyes. Carefully, slowly, she reached up to kiss him. His lips touched hers and he nibbled at them until she couldn't stand the temptation any longer. She opened her mouth and flicked her tongue across his.

With a groan, he pulled her close and lowered her to the bed. He rose above her, his blue eyes troubled and shining with passion. "You're going to regret this," he warned. "You're just reaching out for comfort." He shook his head slightly. "Stop now, Allie."

She wrapped her hand around his nape and pulled his head down. "Don't talk," she murmured against his lips.

When she lifted her gaze, she caught that expression again. That tender indulgence that turned his sharply defined features into a thing of exquisite beauty.

He took a long breath and closed his eyes.

He was so strong. His determination and focus were legendary. Mitch Decker never faltered.

She'd hoped he wanted her as much as she wanted

him. When he'd opened the bathroom door and walked out in nothing but his slacks, his shoulders and torso bare, she'd felt her insides melt in anticipation.

Her heart fluttering with fear and disappointment, Allie steeled herself for rejection. He would be noble and loyal to Joe and refuse to take advantage of her.

She endured his one last searching look, and waited for him to pull away.

Then, to her surprise, his eyelids dipped down over his incredible blue eyes, he lowered his head and took her mouth with a wild thoroughness that left her breathless. His tongue slid between her parted lips and explored, probed and delved in an erotic imitation of the sexual dance to come. Then he rained kisses across her cheeks and chin.

All the while his hands worked magic on her skin. She felt fire-like sparks wherever he touched. His hand slipped up under the butterfly T-shirt and caressed her breast, teasing it taut, then slid down to spread his fingers over her belly.

She moved closer, pressing against him, feeling his thick, hot desire against her thighs. She moaned, responding to his heavy need. She reached for the buttons on her jeans, and he brushed her hands away and undid them himself. She arched, making it easier for him to slide them off. Then he stood, his hands at the zipper of his slacks.

"Allie?"

She reached for the zipper. His hands covered hers, so she pulled away and drew her T-shirt off over her head and unsnapped the silly red bra while he rid himself of his pants.

When Mitch lay down again, his hot body burning

into her side, she realized she'd been cold and empty for a long time.

Hesitantly, she stretched out her hand, craving the silky hardness of him against her palm.

When she touched him, he gasped and moaned against her mouth, his reaction an aphrodisiac that sent her closer and closer to the point of no return. She caressed him shyly, marveling that every part of him was so perfect.

He bent and took the tip of one breast in his mouth as his hands spanned her waist and slid around to support her back.

His fingers grazed her scars, startling her.

"Damn!" he said, going still as a stone.

Her heart thudded against her chest. "Mitch—" she whispered raggedly.

He lifted his head. His electric-blue eyes, which had been soft and dark with passion just seconds before, now blazed with shock.

With almost no effort, he turned her onto her stomach.

"Don't, Mitch," she cried, struggling. "It's nothing."

Mitch's mouth went dry as he caught her wrists, refusing to allow her to turn over to hide the scars from her bullet wounds. He cursed under his breath as he stared at the awful legacy the FBI had left her. No wonder she wanted to be as far away from everything associated with the Bureau as possible.

"How did you survive?" His voice was gravely, harsh.

She pulled against his grip on her wrists until he was afraid he would hurt her. "Be still."

"No. I don't want you looking at them," she muttered. "They're ugly, but they're healed."

"Do they hurt?"

She shook her head, her coppery hair sliding across her naked back. "Mitch, please, let me go."

"Lie still," he whispered. "I don't want to hurt you." He kept his grip on her wrists as he bent to kiss the awful places where bullets had penetrated her body, nearly killing her.

Allie moaned when his lips touched her damaged skin.

"I wish I could kiss them away." He pressed his mouth against each puckered circle and felt a fine trembling start in her. "I should have been there to stop them."

He slid his tongue across the expanse of creamy skin between the two scars, his head filled with colliding visions of her—facedown on the bloodstained Italian marble floor, and beneath him now, surrounded by white sheets and shadows.

Letting go of her wrists, he raised himself so she could turn. Her emerald eyes glittered like gems in the fading light, her lips were parted, her breathing rapid.

He eased himself between her legs. "You're beautiful. You must know that. I'm so sorry, Allie—"

"Don't you dare!"

He stopped, surprised.

"Don't be sorry. Not for anything. Not tonight." Allie blinked away tears. The tenderness with which he'd caressed the awful scars had been almost more than she could take. He was the most beautiful, the strongest, the gentlest man she'd ever known.

And if he were anyone but who he was, she'd believe he loved her.

She ran her hands up his sleek forearms to his rock-hard biceps and over his collarbone down to his chest, where soft hair dusted the steel bands of muscles that crisscrossed his chest.

His skin was velvet draped over granite. She lifted her head to brush her lips across his nipple, and heard his breath rasp in his throat.

The intensity of his response fed hers, and she arched toward him.

"Be sure, Allie," he said in a harsh whisper. "Tomorrow, you'll still believe I'm your enemy. I'll stop now." He leaned over her, his arms on either side of her head, his face no more than an inch from hers.

Allie's senses were exploding like fireworks. She was consumed with desire—close, so very close to that elusive peak that she'd reached only a couple of times in her life.

His body covered her, deliciously heavy, and she could feel him pulsing against the juncture of her thighs.

"Don't you dare stop," she whispered against his lips. "Please."

He drew in a sharp breath and slid his hand down her belly and lower, to touch her.

Her breath caught sharply when he tentatively caressed her with one finger. "Oh—" she gasped. "Mitch—now."

He lifted himself and slid forward, pushing carefully, agonizingly slowly, into her. She'd never felt so wanton, so sexual, so alive.

She arched to meet him, knowing she was more than ready. He plunged and as he did, he kissed her, matching thrust for thrust. Allie held on to him for dear life as he lifted his head to watch her. He found her rhythm and took her up, up and over the edge.

She fell into his eyes and drowned in electric-blue climax.

Chapter Ten

Dan Withers walked straight into the evidence room. He'd done a few favors for the sergeant who worked the evening shift, so Ramsey occasionally let him get by without signing in and out. Ramsey understood that undercover cops couldn't always get the supplies they needed through regular means. Money was tight all over. Who would miss a few ounces of cocaine or bags of grass?

Ramsey glanced at him with narrowed eyes, but Withers knew what he was thinking. If he didn't know anything, he couldn't testify to anything.

Withers ran through the shelves until he came to the evidence box for Joseph Barnes's murder case. He pulled on a pair of exam gloves, and shuffled through the stack of crime scene photos, ignoring the ones of Barnes and his wife. He was looking for a couple of very specific pictures.

He dealt out the two that showed a shoe print on the Italian tile floor of Barnes's house, then dug out the transfer sheet the crime scene investigator had used to lift the print off the tile.

Reaching under his jacket, he pulled out two photos

and a transfer sheet that he had created earlier at Barnes's former home. Carefully, he copied the information from each of the evidence photos to the new photo, then inserted the new ones into the stack. He did the same with the new transfer sheet.

Then he replaced the vial he'd taken yesterday, the one with Allison Barnes's name on it.

He placed the bag back on the shelf, pocketed the pictures, and left, not even acknowledging Sergeant Ramsey, who was still reading his magazine.

Driving to Decker's apartment, Withers thought about the man he was about to frame with planted evidence. He was a decent guy. Withers had nothing against him personally. In fact, Decker had lent his team's expertise to Withers on a couple of cases. On one occasion, Withers had saved the FBI agent's skin.

But Decker had a fatal flaw. He'd risen fast, mostly on his merit, but also aided by his mentor, Special Agent in Charge Joe Barnes. That didn't happen often in the FBI, but when it did, it always created tension.

Decker had enemies, and one of those enemies was setting him up.

Withers shrugged to himself. No skin off his nose. Withers was an expert at sneaking around unobserved, and this time he was being paid well for his expertise.

Within less than a half hour, Withers had slipped into Decker's apartment, found his auxiliary weapon and replaced it with one containing traces of Mrs. Barnes's blood. He'd also planted a forged receipt in the bottom of a cluttered desk drawer. Then he replaced the shoes he'd taken earlier from Decker's closet and doctored carefully with Allison Barnes's blood.

Back in his car, he felt the satisfaction of a job well

done. Twenty K. Not bad for a night's work, Withers thought. He pulled out his cell phone and dialed a number. "It's done. You got your evidence against Decker."

"No names! No names! You took care of it all?"

Withers smiled at Irby's paranoia. The sweaty lawyer was probably wiping his face with his handkerchief right now.

Irby was too self-involved to recognize how good Withers was at his job. "All. Although I'm not sure how you're going to explain why Decker would shoot Barnes's wife."

"That's not your concern." Irby's voice had turned squeaky. "Stop using names or I'll hang up."

"No problem. Now, about my—" He paused meaningfully. If the guy wanted to play secret agent, Withers would play along.

"Okay. Okay. Your compensation will be forthcoming."

For a second, Withers was tempted to blurt out Irby's name just for meanness, but it'd be a shame if the pompous ass had a heart attack before Withers got his money. So Withers kept quiet.

"I'll look forward to my compensation," he mocked. The phone went dead.

Withers allowed himself a small smile. This case was turning out to be quite lucrative. Maybe he'd retire once it was done.

ALLIE HELD OUT her glass for Joe to pour her more wine. His hand shook as he held his own glass up. "To finally laying the past to rest and to a new future."

The bell-like sound of the glasses clinking together echoed around her as she forced herself to smile. Joe seemed nervous, and his toast was odd.

"Joe, is something wrong? What do you mean, laying the past to rest?"

The lines that creased his cheeks grew deeper as he dropped his gaze to his glass. "No. Nothing's wrong. I just have a feeling things are going to change. I have something to tell you." He smiled. "Something you'll be happy about. Something we've both wanted for a long time." He held his glass higher. "Now, let's drink our toast."

Allie lifted her glass just as the doorbell rang.

Joe started and a few bloodred drops of wine spilled onto the granite countertop.

"I wonder who that is," she said, rising.

"Allie—wait." Joe put down his glass. "Let me get it."

But he was standing on the other side of the big island in the middle of the kitchen.

She waved her hand at him as she walked down the hall, her heels clicking on the Italian marble floor. Switching the wineglass from her right hand to her left, she reached for the doorknob.

A dark shape stood just beyond the circle of light cast by the light behind her.

"Hello, Allie. Is Joe home?"

The visitor stepped into the light. Allie was surprised when she realized who it was. "Yes. Yes, he is. Come in." Before she could even step aside, the dark shape glided around her like black mist, trailing a familiar scent in his wake.

"Hello, Joe."

Allie turned to see that Joe had followed her down the hall.

Joe's eyes met hers and her heart leapt into her

throat at his look of calm certainty. She opened her mouth, but she couldn't speak.

Joe said something, and the dark shadow replied, then lifted his hand.

Light flashed.

MITCH WAS REACHING for Allie before he woke completely. Her soft, distressed sounds had penetrated his sleep. Her cheeks were wet.

"Hey, hey," he whispered, pulling her warm, soft body into the shelter of his. "Allie, wake up."

"No, no, no," she mumbled and stiffened.

He couldn't understand most of what she said. "You're having a bad dream. Shh." He pushed the fiery tangles of hair back from her face and touched her cheek.

She winced and pushed against him, then opened her eyes. For an instant, she was still caught in the dream. Mitch held her as she pulled herself out of sleep and into wakefulness.

Her eyes focused on him. "Mitch?"

He pulled her closer. "It's okay. You were having a bad dream."

She gasped and pulled away. "Oh!" She pushed her hair out of her face, then put her hand over her mouth. "I watched him shoot Joe, and I—couldn't do anything."

Mitch saw the horror in her eyes and his pulse raced. He sat up and leaned against the wall. "Come here." He held out his arms. "Tell me about it."

She stared at him, shock and grief clouding her eyes. After a moment, she moved into the circle of his arms, pulling the sheet with her.

Her body felt small and delicate this morning, unlike last night when she'd met him as an equal, giving and taking, seducing and being seduced.

Mitch drove the erotic thoughts from his brain. The night and his self-indulgence were over. This morning, Allie needed his strength and focus.

And he needed her memories. He needed to hear about her dream before the light of morning burned it away.

She laid her head against his shoulder, close enough that the faint warm scent of her hair surrounded him.

"The man at the door spoke to me. He asked if Joe was home. Then he moved around me. There was something in the air, something sharp, biting." She shook her head. "I can't remember."

"Don't worry about it. Just keep talking."

"Joe spoke—and then—" A tear welled and spilled over and rolled down her cheek.

"Allie, what did Joe say?"

She closed her eyes, and two more tears spilled out. Mitch's fingers twitched to wipe them away. His heart ached to promise her she'd never have to cry again, but he knew that was an empty promise.

"Think, Allie. What did Joe say?"

"He said, 'I'm not changing my mind.'"

Disappointment flooded Mitch. It was the same thing he'd heard Joe say to Hangout. Had Allie incorporated what Mitch had told her about that overheard conversation into her dream? "Are you sure you heard him say that?"

"I could hear his voice in my head."

"Is that everything?"

She wiped her face with both hands and the sheet slipped, revealing her perfect, creamy breasts.

Mitch kept his gaze on her face, swallowing hard against the instantaneous response of his body to the loveliness displayed before him.

"He called me Allie." When she lowered her hands, her eyes were bright and anxious. "The man at the door called me Allie. That means it was someone who knew me well." Her smile faded. "A friend." Her voice was suddenly brittle.

Mitch nodded. "Right." He took her hand. "I'm sorry, Allie, but we always figured you wouldn't have let him in if you hadn't known him. How many people called you Allie?"

"Joe was the first," she said sadly. "My father had always called me Allison. Only people who knew me well, whom we both knew. They'd hear Joe call me Allie and pick it up."

That was exactly what Mitch had done. Joe had always talked about "Allie." It seemed natural for Mitch to use Joe's affectionate nickname. It fit her better than the more formal Allison.

"Do you remember anything about his height or size? Could you see his face?"

She shook her head. "The hallway was dark, and the shape glided by me as if it were floating, like smoke. I can't remember anything else."

"Okay. That was good." He smiled and touched her cheek. "Don't worry. It'll come back."

A glimmer of fear darkened her eyes as she nodded. "I know it will. It has to. But it scares me."

It scared him, too. It was hard enough, fighting an unknown enemy, not knowing whom to trust. But Mitch had a feeling when the face of the enemy was known, it would be a fight to the death. His hand clenched into a fist.

"Mitch, I've got to go back to the house."

His reaction was as immediate and strong as it had been the first time she'd mentioned it. "No!"

She stared at him for an instant, then pulled away, reaching for her clothes.

He rolled off the bed and pulled on his slacks, thinking about his knee-jerk reaction. He rubbed the back of his neck and searched for an explanation that would convince Allie.

"It makes perfect sense," Allie said. "I want to walk down the hallway, where it happened." She tilted her head—that little frown wrinkling her brow, her face pale but determined. "I want to put my hand on the brass knob and turn it. Open the door—" Her hands began to shake, and she gripped her elbows.

Mitch couldn't stand the thought of her doing those things over again. "No. Look at you. It terrifies you just thinking about it. Besides, it's too dangerous to go there. Someone might be watching the house, expecting you to do that very thing."

"It's dangerous everywhere. That's not an excuse." She glared at him. "Why don't you want me to go back there? What's the real reason? Do you think I can't take it? Are you still trying to protect me?" Anger flushed her features. "Well, like I've told you before, don't bother. I don't need protection. I need answers."

She grabbed her shoes and sat down to put them on. "I'll just go by myself."

"The hell you will!" Mitch clenched his fists in helpless frustration.

Allie looked up from tying her shoe. The look on Mitch's face was a look she'd never seen before. He appeared furious, but he had a wild, wary look in his eye, as if he didn't know what to do. The idea that solid, steady Mitch was unsure of something sent a flutter of fear through her.

"What's the real problem, Mitch? Why are you avoiding the one place where we might really be able to find answers? The therapist kept trying to take me back there in my mind, made me go over and over the little bit I remembered. Do you think I can't face it? Well, I can."

"I know you think you can."

She stood and stuck her face in his. "Then let's go. You don't have to worry about me. I'm not afraid of seeing where Joe and I were shot."

His head jerked and his gaze darted beyond her. Then he turned away, reaching for his T-shirt.

She stared at the tense, bunched muscles of his back. "Oh, my God," she whispered. She put her hand out, her fingers brushing his spine, but he tensed even more and stepped away to pull the T-shirt over his head.

"Oh, Mitch. I'm sorry. You were there. You saw Joe lying on the floor. And me." Tears crowded into her throat.

He'd gotten to the scene at the same time as the EMTs, so she knew what he'd seen. She'd seen the same thing eight years before in the driveway of her father's home.

She understood the tragic helplessness, the impotent fury and fear, the uncontrollable urge to reach out and touch the person, as if that would send life flowing magically back into his body.

Allie knew that whatever she managed to remember about the night Joe was killed, she did not own the awful picture that had met Mitch when he'd gotten to his friend's house.

Mitch had to face her. He couldn't be such a coward that he couldn't look her in the eye and face his fear. He lifted his gaze to find her sea-foam-green eyes awash with tears—for him.

He nodded. "You're right. We have to go there. But we should wait until dark."

"Why? If someone is watching, they're not going to go home at night. Besides, we can go in through the back under the cover of the trees. I still have a key."

"THANK YOU for seeing me," Grant Irby said, smoothing his tie as he pushed his portly form into one of Deputy Assistant Director Conover's side chairs. His neck itched as a drop of sweat ran down to dampen his tight collar. He dug a handkerchief out of his coat pocket.

Conover raised an arrogant eyebrow and then glanced pointedly at his desk clock. "Well? What's this information that was too important to talk about on the phone? I have a meeting in twelve minutes."

Irby shifted and blotted the back of his neck. Why did people keep their offices so warm? It was summer. He folded his handkerchief and took a deep breath.

"I have information that links Special Agent Mitchell Decker to Joe Barnes's murder."

Conover's face actually turned pale. Irby suppressed a smile. Now he had the deputy assistant director's attention.

"Decker? Have you lost your mind? What information?"

Irby smoothed his tie again. "We received an anonymous tip that the police might want to look at Decker's apartment. I obtained a search warrant based on the fact that he is AWOL and harboring a fugitive."

Conover wiped a hand over his face and stared at Irby through his fingers. "An anonymous tip. Have you executed the warrant?"

"His apartment is being searched now. If the evidence is there, the police will issue a warrant for his arrest."

"I know your responsibility is to investigate Joe's murder, but Special Agent Decker is known for his integrity and high moral standards." Conover stood and pointed his finger at Irby, his color returning to his face.

"I swear, Irby, if this is a hoax, your job is going to be on the line."

Irby swallowed. Conover had never liked Decker. Irby was certain of that. At the very least, he'd expected an "atta boy" for following up so promptly on the tip.

Conover didn't sit back down. He walked over to his office door and opened it.

Irby pried himself out of the chair and walked to the door. "Remember, sir, I'm available and eager to cooperate. Just call me. I'll do anything."

Conover shot Irby a disgusted look as he pushed the door closed. Irby had to scurry to keep it from hitting him in the butt.

THE HOUSE had the hollow, sad look that empty houses get. The grounds were unkempt and bedraggled. The shock of seeing the beautiful house that she'd spent so much time on in such a state of neglect really slammed Allie in the face. Mitch had told her the house was still on the market, but the reality of seeing it in such disrepair was heartbreaking. During the seventeen months she'd spent in the Witness Security Program, she hadn't considered the time that had passed. Her life had truly been stolen from her that day.

By the time she'd found the key under a false stone beside the cobblestoned path that wound through the small garden behind the house, she was shaking with trepidation. She was certain of her decision. She knew she had to face what had happened that night in order to remember. But despite her determination, despite her bravado, fear thrummed in her temples as she thought about standing there, reaching for the door-knob.

Her hand shook as she unlocked the side utility door and they slipped into the blackness of the garage under the first floor of the house.

"The stairs are over here," she whispered, then felt silly for whispering. But the dark silence of the house where Joe had died seemed to call for it. She'd walked the dozen or so steps from the utility door to the stairs many times, so she laid her hand on Mitch's left fore-arm to guide him.

He turned his arm and took her hand in his as he moved like a cat burglar, silent and tense. She knew he was holding his weapon in his right hand. Always on guard.

"The same key opens the door at the top of the stairs," she whispered.

"Unlock it and stand to the side, and have your gun ready."

She did as she was told.

When Mitch opened the door into the laundry room off the kitchen, sunlight streaming through windows il-luminated thousands of specks of dust. The brightness was startling after the cloaking darkness of the garage. Allie squinted as Mitch led the way into the kitchen.

The furniture was gone, and the empty house echoed.

Allie walked over to the granite-topped island in the middle of the kitchen. She touched a dark red stain on its surface.

"Joe spilled wine here," she said softly. "That night. He was standing on this side of the island, opening a new bottle, or he'd have gone to the door."

She'd smiled at Joe when he'd told her to wait and let him open the door. At the time, she'd thought it was his natural chivalry and waved away his offer as she hurried down the hall to open the door. Now, she wondered about his nervousness. He'd looked worried. Had he been afraid of who was there?

The scars on her back ached.

Mitch walked across the kitchen to the double doors that opened onto the back patio and peered out.

"You can't see the front from back here," she said, taking a deep breath to calm her suddenly pounding pulse as she turned and looked down the hall to the marble-tiled entryway. "You can see through the window in the den, on the right side of the hall. There are heavy drapes and window shades in there, if no one has taken them down."

"Wait here."

"Mitch, stop doing that. I'll go with you."

They walked down the hall together, Mitch holding his gun in both hands, alert, balanced, ready for the danger he obviously thought lurked in every shadow.

Allie felt the pall of death and tragedy over the house. Maybe it was just because it had been her home, and she had been the victim. But she wondered if the sense of tragic loss was palpable to others. Maybe that's why the house hadn't sold.

Her vision telescoped on the entryway in front of her.

In the dusty light from the transom window, the luxurious blue-veined Italian marble of the floor seemed dull. There were no lights, of course, and the gossip bench that had held the hall phone was gone. In front of her, the double mahogany carved door with its faceted, beveled glass accents was cloaked in shadow.

Although her tennis shoes made no noise, her ears echoed with the memory of the light click of her heels on the marble floor that night. She'd worn a green silk lounging robe and had carried her wineglass with her to the door. She remembered switching the glass from her right hand to her left then reaching for the doorknob. Her fingers twitched, recalling the cold brass.

Mitch stopped her with a gesture, interrupting her mesmerizing recollections. "In here." He pulled her into Joe's office.

The room was as dark as it had always been. Joe had liked the dark leather chairs and heavy drapes. He'd said that open windows distracted him when he was thinking about a problem.

Mitch looked down at her, pulling her attention from the empty space where Joe's desk had sat. "Are you okay?"

She nodded, giving him a small smile. "I'm fine. Joe wouldn't let me redo his den when I did the rest of the house. He loved this room."

Mitch's gaze softened. "I know. He even kept brandy and glasses in his desk."

"He was a gentleman."

Yes, he was. Mitch stepped over to the window. "I want to check out the street."

He lifted the edge of the dusty blinds with the barrel of his gun and peered out. It looked like a typical quiet day in the neighborhood. In the green area beyond the circular drive in front of the house sat a crooked For Sale sign.

There were a few cars parked on the street. One, in front of a high-columned, three-story brick home, had a real estate logo stuck to the driver's side door frame.

"There's a real estate car a few doors down. We need to hurry, in case they're coming here."

A movement farther down the street caught his attention. A utility van pulled to the curb several houses down. He watched the van for several seconds, feeling uneasy.

"What is it? What else do you see?" Allie had picked up on his increased tension.

"A van just stopped down the street."

"It's probably the cable company, D.C. Cable. There have always been problems in this neighborhood. They were out here at least once a week when—when I lived here."

That was the name on the van. But Allie's words didn't erase his unease. "I don't like it. Anyone watching the neighborhood would know that and could use a similar truck as cover." The back door of the van opened and a man in a uniform with a tool belt pulled out a roll of cable and began unrolling it toward the house. A woman opened the front door and spoke to the man.

Mitch watched, frowning, then let the blinds fall back into place. "Come on," he said to Allie. "Let's get this over with. We're too exposed here. Too vulnerable."

Allie's gaze met his. She took a deep breath and clasped her hands. "Okay. I'm going to walk down the hall and open the door." Her voice sounded brittle.

Mitch touched her arm. "Want me to walk with you?"

She shook her head distractedly, her attention already on the foyer as she stepped out into the hall. "When the bell rang, Joe was about to tell me something. Something that would make me happy, he said."

Mitch followed her, listening to her words, trying to picture what she was describing.

But when he glanced back toward the kitchen, his mind's eye pictured Joe sprawled on the floor, blood everywhere. The blood was gone from the floor, but Mitch's gaze followed the natural arc he knew the blood spatter had taken. There, exactly where he'd seen it that night, its obscene blackness marring the elegant wallpaper, was a graphic reminder of Joe's violent death. The cleaning team had missed it.

He glanced back at Allie, hoping she hadn't noticed the blood. She hadn't. Her attention was on the mahogany doors. She walked slowly toward them.

Again, Mitch's imagination filled in the details from the picture that was burned indelibly into his brain. Allie, face down, her blood spreading to stain the floor and soak her hair. Her hand had been stretched toward the phone, a tragic reminder that she'd almost reached it by the time the bullets slammed into her back.

Before he'd had a chance to fully process the horror of the scene, the EMTs had blocked her from his view as they bent over her, working against the clock to save her life. But his brain had been faster than high-speed film. The image would be with him forever.

His cell phone rang.

He jumped, but Allie didn't react. He grabbed it before it could ring a second time.

"Don't open the door," he cautioned Allie as he looked at the display and saw that the calling number was blocked. He pressed the answer button but didn't speak.

"Decker?"

It was Jack. He sounded cautious.

"Yeah?"

"Where are you?"

Mitch didn't like the tone of Jack's voice. Something had happened. "Joe's house. What's happened?"

"There's a warrant for your arrest."

Jack was speaking so low it was hard to hear him.

"Warrant? For what?"

Jack paused. "The murder of Joe Barnes."

"What?" Shock reverberated through Mitch's brain. For a split second, his total attention was on the phone. Too slowly, he processed Jack's words and forced them into context.

Murder. Joe Barnes.

A movement caught his attention.

Standing directly in front of the double doors, like she must have that night, Allie turned the doorknob.

"Allie!" Alarm signals buzzed in Mitch's head. He started toward her. "Don't open—"

She swung the door wide.

Something flashed beyond her.

She dropped to the floor like a discarded rag.

"Allie!"

A shadowed figure pointed the oddly shaped weapon he'd just used on Allie at Mitch.

Mitch dropped the phone and fired, all in one motion, but the nanosecond of time he'd wasted in horrified shock as he'd watched Allie collapse had given the attacker enough time to hit him.

He didn't feel a bullet. He felt a slight pressure in his

chest, then nothing. He watched his gun drop, and then his body collapsed beneath him.

He tried to dive toward Allie, but his limbs weren't obeying his brain.

Then his muscles spasmed in unbelievable pain and a bomb exploded in his head.

His last thought was that he'd just witnessed the thing he'd been so afraid of since Allie had come to him.

He'd just watched her die.

IT WASN'T UNTIL the shoe connected with his ribs for the third time that Mitch realized he was still alive. The realization wasn't a conscious thought. Rather it was a visceral, gradual awareness growing out of the red-tinged blackness in his head.

As the black faded to foggy gray and before any coherent thought could form, every muscle in his body seized in bone-cracking, nerve-shattering pain. He did his best, but his best wasn't good enough to stop the tendons in his body from contracting until he was curled into a fetal ball.

In some part of his brain not lit by pain, he heard the man with the shoe talking, but nothing made sense. Agony dominated his being.

Somewhere beyond the conscious, he felt another pain, an anguish that, when he identified it, would seize his heart and rip it into pieces; but his brain wasn't working any better than his body. That pain had a form, a name more precious than his own life, but he couldn't quite grasp it.

"—intruder reported by—something wrong—acts like he's been—"

As the unbearable pain dulled to a merely screaming agony, and the tendons eased their punishing grip on his muscles, certain words the person was saying began to make sense.

He couldn't string the words together, though. They hit his brain at random.

"—has a weapon—no wallet—bring him in. No sign of—front door wide—cap with a few long dark hairs—"

A wordless cry built in the back of Mitch's throat, but his lungs wouldn't take in enough air to breathe, much less scream.

With a superhuman effort, Mitch forced his muscles to obey his brain's commands. He managed to unclench his fists and stretch his legs. Then the cramping attacked him again. He rolled up into a ball until it eased.

"—call coming in. Let's go—station. Help—to the car."

Mitch fought his way up past the pain again and heard another voice.

"Yes, sir. A stun gun or Taser."

He felt hands under his armpits, dragging him, and saw a uniformed police car. Since his limbs wouldn't work and his brain was still fading in and out, he didn't try to fight. He figured he and Allie could be in worse hands than the police.

Allie. The anguish he'd felt beyond the physical had a face—a beautiful, beloved face. Where was she? He tried to say her name, but all he could manage was a choked cry that even in his fogged state he knew wasn't a word.

By the time the car pulled in at the police station, Mitch's muscles had stopped drawing up and were merely twitching uncontrollably, and his tongue felt less like a piece of cotton and more like a tongue.

The young officer opened the car door and reached in.

"Think you can stand now, buddy?" he said, dragging Mitch up by the collar. Mitch tried to move his arms and realized he was handcuffed.

He stood shakily, his knees threatening to buckle and his head spinning dizzily. Nausea stuck in the back of his throat, along with all the questions he wanted to ask. But he didn't dare speak, for fear of throwing up.

He concentrated on putting one foot in front of the other without losing control of his muscles. The officer whose hand clutched his collar was walking too fast. Mitch stumbled, lurched. Every molecule of his dazed and throbbing brain concentrated on moving his legs. Finally, after what seemed like hours, the officer dropped him into a straight-backed chair in an interrogation room and stood over him.

"All right, buddy. What's your name and what were you doing in that house?"

"Back off, *buddy.*"

A familiar voice. Mitch squeezed his eyes shut and tried to focus on the source. Fighting double vision and a foggy haze, he met Jack O'Hara's gray eyes.

"Jack," he croaked, struggling to sit up straight. "Al—"

"Get him some water, and call a doctor. Now!"

The officer glanced at a second person who'd come into the room, then Decker heard the door open and close.

"Decker? Can you understand me?" Jack sat down across from him, peering at him with a worried frown.

What the hell had happened? He nodded and concentrated on lifting one hand to rub his burning eyes.

"How's Allie?" he managed, although his tongue felt thick and stiff. "They—hit her—first."

His eyes were no better for being rubbed, and his arm felt like he'd carried a two-ton weight. He let his hand drop to the table.

Jack's frown deepened. "Decker, listen to me. You were at Joe's house. I heard the shots through your cell phone. Before I could get there, some real estate agent who apparently wanted to show the house reported an intruder, and a couple of D.C.'s finest showed up and hauled you in. The locals have secured the scene and are going over it to see what happened."

The more Jack talked, the more Mitch understood. Someone handed Jack a cup of water and Jack pushed it toward Mitch. With intense concentration, Mitch was able to raise the cup without spilling too much water. The liquid felt cool in his mouth. He struggled to swallow without choking. He coughed a couple of times.

"We think you were hit by a stun gun, maybe a liquid Taser. We should have a doctor here soon to check you out."

Mitch opened his mouth but Jack kept talking.

"Did you see anything? Do you know who did this to you?"

Mitch shook his head. "Damn it, Jack," he muttered thickly. "Allie!"

Jack dropped his gaze to Mitch's hands.

Mitch felt the unbearable pain rending his heart. He was right. It was worse than the muscle cramps or the blinding headache. Much worse.

God, please don't let her be dead.

Unable to speak, Mitch reached out and grabbed Jack's wrist. Jack didn't try to pull away, even though Mitch knew his grip was no stronger than a newborn's.

Jack met his gaze and Mitch saw his answer before he spoke. Shaking his head jerkily, he tried to deny the truth.

"She wasn't at the scene, Mitch. Her baseball cap was there, in the doorway, a few hairs caught in it." Jack moved his hand from Mitch's nerveless grip and gripped his shoulder.

"Allie's missing."

Chapter Eleven

"Mrs. Barnes." The voice had droned in Allie's head for what seemed like hours. She wanted to slap it away like an annoying bee, but her arms were too heavy and her head hurt.

"Mrs. Barnes."

She tried to think, but her brain felt murky and slow, and her body ached everywhere. The last thing she remembered was opening that door. Again.

Her heart lurched and her thoughts sharpened to horrifying clarity. It had been just like before. She'd opened her front door and confronted a killer.

Oh, dear God—Mitch! Had they killed him, just like they'd killed Joe? A loss so profound, so deep her body couldn't contain it, filled her every pore.

He couldn't be dead. He was younger, stronger than Joe had been. Mitch was always on guard, his instincts honed to razor sharpness.

If he were dead, then she must be, too, because she couldn't live without him.

"Mrs. Barnes!"

"What?" she snapped. Only what came out wasn't snappish. It was barely a squeak. Her lips wouldn't form the *wh* sound and her tongue wouldn't close on the *T,* so all she'd managed was something that sounded pathetically like *ha.*

A chuckle answered her. "So you are beginning to shake off the effects of the Taser."

Peering through slitted eyelids, she explored her surroundings. She was in the back seat of a car. The odor of expensive leather mixed with men's cologne and tobacco filled her nostrils.

Sitting next to her was a small chunky man, with a swarthy balding dome of a head and dark brown eyes. She couldn't keep her eyes open though, because sunlight seeping through the tinted windows sent flashes of pain through her temples.

She tried to lift her arm again and found that she could, but it ached so much it didn't seem worth it.

"It's time for you to wake up. From what I understand about Tasers, you should be over the worst of the muscle spasms by now. Why don't you sit up? Would you like some water?"

Tasers?

Her still foggy brain tried to grasp what the man was saying. She knew what Tasers were. She'd seen them in her training at Quantico. There was something important about them that she should remember. Something vitally important.

Allie tested her limbs and discovered she was slumped ungracefully in the back seat of a Lincoln Town Car. She pushed upright, ignoring her protesting calves and thighs. Then she lifted her aching hand to push her hair out of her face.

Carefully running her tongue along her lips, she was relieved to discover she could feel them. Then she opened her mouth, and with a great deal of effort and concentration, she asked the question that was burning inside her.

"Where—is Mitch?"

The man, who held a long, unlit cigar, waved his free hand. "Your friend, Special Agent Decker? Last I saw, he was still on the floor of your home, likely in terrible pain."

Tasers didn't cause permanent damage. That was the important thing. Mitch wasn't dead.

"You left him there? Alive?" She held her breath, needing to hear this stranger assure her that Mitch was okay, that she hadn't lost him, too.

She'd lost so much when her father had been murdered. Then when she'd woken up in the hospital to find that Joe was dead, Allie's heart had shattered. Yet in the past few days, she'd discovered that her wounded heart still had room for love.

"We were in a hurry, and you were the objective, not him."

Tears stung her eyes. "Thank God." Mitch was all right. He would find her. And he would be so angry. He'd warned her how important it was to listen to him.

Allie, don't open the door. She'd heard his cell phone ring, heard his worried voice, but she'd been too buried in memories for his words to sink in. As she'd approached the door, as she had that awful night, she'd deliberately tried to take herself out of the present and into the past. Her pulse had thrummed in anticipation as she'd turned the cold brass knob.

She'd expected to feel a rush of adrenaline when she swung the door open. She'd hoped that in her mind's eye, she would see a man standing there, a man she recognized.

But all she had seen was sunlight reflecting off a large weapon. Before she could react, something had hit her, sending numbness and paralyzing pain along every muscle and nerve in her body. She'd felt herself falling, as if she were sinking into deep water—down, down, down.

"Mrs. Barnes, try to concentrate on the present." The man's voice broke into her thoughts. "Here. Drink this."

She blinked. He looked impatient as he held out a small bottle of water.

What were his words? *She was the objective, not Mitch.* "Why do you want me? Who are you?"

She squinted at him, racking her damaged memory for even the tiniest twinge of familiarity. She found nothing. Either her brain was totally fried or she had never seen this man before.

"My name is Carmine Bongiovi."

Bongiovi. Allie forgot her pain. She pressed her fingers against her hazy eyes, and studied the man with whom her husband had supposedly worked.

"I don't know you," she said, accepting the bottle of water from him. She had to concentrate to hold on to it.

Bongiovi's eyes glittered in the dim interior of the car. "No. We never met. So did running a repeat of the night your husband was murdered jog your memory?"

"No." She shook her head. "Why? Do you expect me to tell you who was at the door that night?" She would have laughed if she'd had the strength.

"No, no. I expect you to remember."

Allie frowned at him. *He knew who the killer was.* The answer settled over her with a certainty that made her skin tighten in apprehension and excitement.

She leaned back against the leather seat and pressed her fingers to her temples, feigning more pain than she actually felt, hoping to milk his disingenuous solicitousness for a few more minutes while she gathered her thoughts. "I don't understand."

"I was hoping you'd have your memories back by now. Hoping that being in your house would help." He looked at the tip of his cigar.

"You were watching the house? Waiting for us?"

"Sure. Made sense that you'd show up eventually." He shifted his attention from her to the driver. "The police done yet?"

Police? What was he talking about? She tried to see through the vehicle's darkened windows, but her eyes were still hazy and the sun on the tinted glass was so bright.

The driver pressed a button on a cell phone and spoke softly for a few seconds. "They're leaving now, sir."

"Finally. There ain't a lot of time, Mrs. Barnes. If you don't remember who murdered your husband in— say—the next couple of hours, I might be forced to kill you."

The frightening words, uttered in Carmine Bongiovi's calm voice, sent terror streaking through Allie like the electric impulse of the Taser, churning her stomach and shooting throbbing pain through her head.

"You already know who killed Joe, don't you? You were probably in on it. So what difference does it make to you whether I remember or not?"

"I know who did it, but I wasn't involved."

Allie stared at Carmine Bongiovi. "I suppose you have a compelling reason why I should believe you?"

"I respected Joe. We had an agreement."

Allie's heart sank at Bongiovi's words. "Are you telling me my husband was working with you?"

"Yes. Are you telling me you don't trust your husband?"

Allie closed her eyes. "I did." Was everyone else right about Joe? Had he been corrupted? And if so by what? Power? Money?

"You should be more loyal. Your husband, he was doing a good thing."

"A good thing? How is working with the major crime kingpin in the city a good thing?"

"I can't say anything more about that."

"If you know who murdered him, why don't you just tell me?" she asked.

Bongiovi twirled his cigar between his fingers. "No, no, no. That ain't going to work. That would be coercion. When you testify, you got to be sincere. Otherwise, you could change your story later, tell 'em I influenced you." He smiled. "When you survived that explosion, it occurred to me that you could be an asset. But you're no good to me unless your memory comes back."

Allie struggled to understand. "I wish you'd stop talking in riddles. Why isn't there a logical way to prove who killed my husband without my testimony?"

Bongiovi's lips turned up in a wry smile. "I could tell the police what I know. But that would incriminate me. Without your eyewitness testimony, nobody's going to believe me, because of my—shall we say—unsavory past."

It was common knowledge that Bongiovi had moved in and taken over the power in the criminal underworld of D.C. during the past eight years. He had his hand in many legitimate businesses, but he was also known to be involved in drug importation and distribution, scams involving real estate and taxes, racketeering and money laundering. He was the kingpin.

She thought about Mitch's certainty that the killer was connected to someone high up in the government. She remembered his gentle but probing questions, and she tried to think like Mitch would think, ask the questions he would ask.

First and most importantly, how would her identification of the murderer help Bongiovi? He obviously hoped to use her knowledge against the killer.

"You want something from me," she said. "Well, I want something from you, too. You said Joe was working with you. On what?"

The little man sighed. "I like your style, Mrs. Barnes. You got guts. Back in the day, I was single, ambitious. Nothing was more important than money. Now I'm a married man." He spread his hands and shrugged.

Fred's words echoed in her ears. *He's got kids. A pretty wife. Grooming his cousin to take over.*

"You're trying to get out. So Joe was—"

"He was fixing me up with a brand new life. Why would I kill him?"

"A new life? How could Joe—" *A new life.* Of course. She better than anyone knew what that meant. Her pulse sped up. That had to be it. Fred Scarbrough had said Bongiovi was trying to get out of the life.

Suddenly, it all fit together. She knew what Joe had been doing. The truth slammed into her like a fist. The late nights. The hours in his study. His obsession with her father's murder.

Anguish gripped her heart like a fist. Impotent rage

boiled up inside her. "Oh, my God, you murdered my father."

If she thought it would do any good, she'd attack him with her bare hands. The image of Bongiovi crumpling as she raked him raw with her fingernails made her feel better.

But she'd be foolish to think she could overpower him. He had a gun. The bulge beneath his expensive, custom-tailored suit coat was subtle but obvious.

She fought the automatic sting of tears that accompanied any thought of her father, and straightened her back. More than ever before, she had to draw on her FBI training. She had to act and think like an agent, not like a grieving daughter or a sad widow.

She folded her arms and glared at him. "You killed my father in cold blood to secure your place as the new underworld kingpin, didn't you? And for some reason Joe was willing to help you. You want out. You've got incriminating evidence against someone important that you want to exchange for protection. So why not just go ahead and testify?"

Bongiovi turned his head and looked out the car window. "I told you. You're the only eyewitness. I need your testimony. The guy who killed Joe has certain knowledge that could put me away for a long, long time. I have two daughters, Mrs. Barnes. I'd like them to know their *papà* as an honest, hard-working businessman."

Allie shrugged. "Well, I can't tell you who was on the other side of that door. All I can see is a dark shape. Very dark, very powerful."

The man collapsed back into the butter-colored leather seat, his face red, his upper lip gleaming with moisture, muttering a string of expletives in what sounded like Italian.

He was bursting with the knowledge, almost apoplectic with the need to blurt out the name. Allie could feel his anticipation in the air.

But she knew he was right, even though his reasons were not the same as hers.

She needed to remember on her own because she wouldn't feel complete until she owned the memories of that awful night. She couldn't move forward until she could lay her past to rest.

"I can't even imagine who it could be," she continued, watching him. "That fellow Seacrest, who vowed revenge on everybody in the Bureau? Grant Irby? Frank Conover? Any one of a dozen or more government officials we knew? None of them had any reason to murder Joe."

Bongiovi glanced at his watch without commenting.

His hints and secrets were irritating and frustrating. Allie looked around at the neighborhood where they were parked. "Why are we sitting in your car, Mr. Bongiovi? We're still near my house, aren't we? You're waiting for something."

"Right again, Mrs. Barnes." Bongiovi's lips curled.

A cell phone rang in the front seat. The driver answered, said something, then turned it off. "All clear." He started the car.

"You're taking me back there, aren't you?"

"You need to remember. I need you to. This time, you're going to open the door and see the man who murdered your husband and tried to kill you." He gestured at the driver, who pulled out of their parking place.

"We don't have much time. I'm sure your Mr. Decker has recovered from the effects of the Taser and is doing his best to rescue you. If the police aren't still holding him."

"The police? Why are they holding him?"

Bongiovi smiled. "For your husband's murder. What else?"

"GET HIM OUT of here." Deputy Assistant Director Frank Conover frowned at the assistant district attorney. "The so-called evidence you have is ludicrous. Any rookie CSI could tell it was planted."

The ADA looked chagrined as he held up his hands. "I assure you, Deputy Conover, we're processing his paperwork now."

"I'd suggest you look very closely at the evidence, and try to discover why Grant Irby went to so much trouble to incriminate Special Agent Decker. Our offices will give you our complete cooperation."

The ADA left the interrogation room, and Conover straightened. He turned to Mitch, letting his gaze slide over Mitch's rumpled clothes and up to his face. He shook his head in regret.

"You should have come to me, son. Four days ago, we could have placed Mrs. Barnes in a safe house, and you wouldn't have been vulnerable to Irby's attempt to frame you for Joe's murder. Now the situation has escalated. Your misplaced loyalty to Barnes has placed his widow in more danger. And even though I'm sure the evidence against you will prove to be false, we still have to endure all the tiresome legalities. You'll have to surrender your gun and badge until we can get this straightened out."

Mitch stood. "Yes, sir," he said, trying to relax his clenched jaw. He didn't need his boss to tell him he'd failed to keep Allie safe. He should never have let her talk him into going anywhere near her Georgetown home.

All he wanted to do was get back out there and find Allie before the killer did, if the man didn't already have her. If he did—something niggled at Mitch's brain. He tried to shake off the last mind-numbing effects of the Taser. He was missing an important point.

"I have several meetings I can't get out of," Conover said, "but I want to meet with you before the end of the day. I'll have Sherbourne call you about a time. Also, the U.S. Marshal's Service wants to interview you about Mrs. Barnes. Sherbourne will set that up, too. Stay in contact with him. He's coordinating everything."

Conover put his hand briefly on Mitch's shoulder— the injured one. Mitch grimaced.

"I'm disappointed in you, son. You have more potential than anyone I've seen come up through the ranks in a long while. It's going to take you some time to live this down. Unfortunately, protocol requires that I strongly consider disciplinary action for your insubordination and your failure to disclose your whereabouts and the whereabouts of a known fugitive."

Mitch's frustration level reached detonation stage. In an effort to stay calm, he clenched his fists at his sides. If Conover didn't quit spouting Bureau-speak soon, Mitch was afraid he might add hitting a supervisory federal agent to his laundry list of infractions.

"And O'Hara, I don't know what you think you're accomplishing here, but you need to be back at the division, doing your job."

"Yes, sir."

Conover nodded and adjusted his tie. He apparently didn't see the flash of anger in Jack's eyes or hear the faint mockery in his tone.

"Good. We understand each other."

Conover finally left, and Mitch signed the necessary papers to be released on his own recognizance. Once he exited the police station, Jack O'Hara pulled up to the curb and lowered his driver's side window. "Need a lift?"

Mitch scowled at him. "No. Why aren't you headed back to the office, like Conover said?"

He knew why. Jack had decided Mitch needed a babysitter, and he had taken on the job. As much as Mitch liked and respected Jack, right now the Ice Man was just another hurdle he had to jump. He had to find Allie.

"I thought you might appreciate a *ride.*"

"I'd appreciate you getting back to your job." Mitch glared at his friend, but he went around and climbed in the passenger side of the government issue vehicle.

"Like I said, I thought you'd appreciate a *ride.*"

"I was planning to take a cab."

"Much less efficient." Jack pulled out into traffic. "So where are you headed?"

"To see Carmine Bongiovi. He's right in the thick of this. And right now, he's the only lead I've got. Hangout Hooper said Joe was working for him."

"You knew Joe better than any of us. Do you think he was under the mob's thumb?"

Mitch adjusted his holster so it wasn't scraping the bandage on his shoulder. "I don't know, but there was something bothering him. Allie is convinced he was close to solving her father's murder. She said he never stopped investigating it."

"It's something to think about. That could be why he was killed. There's always been talk about Bongiovi being connected to MacNeal's death. He rose to power over DeSanto at about the same time as MacNeal was murdered. So you think—"

"Bongiovi either killed Joe, or he knows who did. And he could have taken Allie."

"Have you ever seen Bongiovi's house? It's a virtual fortress. If you go there, you'll be walking right into a trap."

Mitch shrugged. That didn't matter. He'd walk straight into hell to save Allie. "I've got to find her."

"So after all the trouble they went through to trace her and try to kill her, why didn't they just shoot you both on the spot?"

Of course. That's what had been eating at the edge of his sluggish brain. "That's it! My brain's still fogged. The man who murdered Joe would have had no reason to leave Allie or me breathing. Yet they stunned us and kidnapped her. She's alive, Jack."

The relief that gushed through Mitch at his realization was as shocking and sudden as a breath of air to a drowning man. He couldn't suppress a choked groan. He pinched his nose, blinking against the sting of tears.

Jack glanced sidelong at him, but didn't comment. He continued driving while Mitch cleared his throat and struggled to regain control. After a few seconds, he spoke.

"Assuming Bongiovi does have her, what does he want from her?"

"Everything we've managed to dig up points to him. Nat's trace of the partial license from the car ended at Bongiovi's door. Hangout worked for Bongiovi. And if we believe what Hangout said, Joe was working with Bongiovi."

Jack nodded. "So Bongiovi could have killed him."

"Problem is, Allie never met him. But she knew the man at the door that night. What's more, he knew her. He called her Allie, not Allison, and not Mrs. Barnes."

"Did she remember that at the house?"

Mitch shook his head. "No. She'd already recalled that much. Today, she walked through her actions of that night, hoping that being there would trigger her memory. But as soon as she opened the door, she was hit by the Taser."

Mitch confronted the sobering image of Allie falling to the marble floor right in front of his eyes. He should have been quicker. He should have been able to get a decent shot off before that damned Taser hit him. Anger boiled inside him. He fisted his hands.

"And you think Bongiovi is responsible. How do we get from him to the killer?"

"Bongiovi's got connections, we know that." Mitch's brain kicked into high gear. "If he's working for whoever murdered Joe, and he wants Allie alive—"

"He could be using her to save his own butt."

"A contact of mine from my undercover days said Bongiovi's looking to get out of the life."

Jack snorted. "He's looking for protection. Or maybe a plea bargain, depending on what he's got on his rap sheet. He's got information. Maybe he even knows who killed Barnes. He's got Allie. So why hasn't he made his move?"

"He needs something else." Even before Mitch finished speaking, the answer hit him like a punch to the gut. "She's the only eyewitness to Joe's murder. His word alone would be hearsay, but with Allie's eyewitness testimony to corroborate his, he could write his own ticket to a quiet life in the suburbs."

"And if the killer knows Bongiovi has Allie—"

"He'll try to kill them both." Mitch had no time to waste. "I've got to find her. Pull over here."

"Boss, you can't handle him alone. You need backup."

"I'll call you if I need you."

Jack stopped the car and stared intently at Mitch. "It would be smart to call in a SWAT team. They can take Bongiovi into custody and rescue Allie."

"We don't know who wants her dead. I can't take a chance with her life." Mitch endured Jack's icy gaze flaying him open, exposing the secret he'd carried in his heart all these years.

After a few seconds, Jack nodded. He understood. "Okay. I hope to hell she's worth it."

Mitch set his mouth. His heart didn't lie. "She is."

"Take the car. We've been testing that prototype digital tracking unit on it. Natasha will trace your every move."

Mitch glanced at his second-in-command. "Giving me your vehicle puts your job in jeopardy."

"I'll tell 'em you pulled a gun on me."

Mitch allowed himself a small smile. "Yeah. The gun I left back at the station," he said wryly.

"I'll request that the local police remain on alert. Tell them it would be too dangerous for them to act before we hear from you." Jack opened the driver's side door.

Mitch got out and walked around the car. "You're a good man."

"Yeah. Good and stupid." Jack punched Mitch in the chest with one finger. "If I don't hear from you in two hours, I'm calling in the cavalry."

"Give me three."

"Nope."

"Jack—"

"Two hours. Try not to get your butt shot off, okay?"

Chapter Twelve

Mitch headed for Custis Memorial Parkway toward Falls Church, Virginia, and the multimillion-dollar mansion owned by Carmine Bongiovi. He'd recovered from the Taser stun, but his heart felt like a hole had been drilled through it. Guilt ate at him like drops of water on limestone, wearing away his veneer of calm and focus.

He never should have let Allie talk him into going to her house. Logic had told him the killer would be lying in wait for her there.

The killer. Who in hell could it be? He went over the short list of possible suspects.

Irby? Bongiovi? Seacrest? Withers? Conover? Some unknown associate of Joe's he'd never met?

As he ticked off the names, his brain argued against each one. Irby might be willing to do anything to get a position with the Bureau, but his attempt to frame Mitch was so glaringly inept that Mitch doubted he could have pulled off a murder. At least not alone.

Allie had never met Bongiovi or Withers, so she wouldn't have known them had they shown up at her door. Seacrest was still in prison, and Conover had no motive. He was the deputy assistant director for criminal investigations, and Joe was too small a fish to have ever represented a threat to Conover's advancement.

That left any one of dozens of people Allie knew. But then, there was the question of motive. Mitch shrugged his shoulders, still tight from the cramping effects of the Taser. There was no way he could figure out who Allie had seen that night. She was the only one who knew.

Jack was right. Bongiovi wanted Allie's eyewitness testimony as insurance. As soon as she remembered, he'd contact the Bureau.

Therefore, Allie still hadn't remembered. Mitch thought about her opening the door, so engrossed in reliving that night that she hadn't heard his warning. If she'd had the opportunity to follow through, if she'd been able to open the door and confront her fear, would her brain have given her the answer?

An uneasy feeling rose like a knot under Mitch's breastbone. His fingers clenched around the steering wheel. His instinct told him he was headed the wrong way.

Mitch shook his head sharply. No. The logical move was to see Bongiovi, offer him protection and vow to somehow find the proof to back up his claim.

But the irritating voice in his head argued with him. Allie would do anything to drag those memories from her uncooperative brain.

And so would Bongiovi. Worry for Allie's safety consumed him.

She'd have recovered from the effects of the Taser by now—and Bongiovi would be doing his best to dig that name from her brain.

Sweat beaded on Mitch's upper lip. How would he do it? Torture? Drugs?

No. The answer was so obvious he couldn't believe he hadn't already thought of it.

Bongiovi would take her back to her house for another walk through.

Mitch took the next exit and stopped. The logical side of his brain was at war with his instinct. Logically, it was hard to imagine that Bongiovi would put himself at that much risk. But he needed Allie's memories.

God, Mitch hated the part of him that was like his father. That inexplicable, unconscious reasoning that made leaps logic couldn't follow. His father had used his ability to ruin people, to collapse companies.

That was why Mitch had always relied on logic, on the steady, slow, step-by-step process of reasoning. He'd done his best to repress the instinctive side of his brain.

The last time he'd let his instinct guide him, Joe had died, and Allie had been grievously injured.

Wiping a hand over his face, Mitch gave in to the grief and guilt for a few seconds, his mind going back to that life-altering moment when he'd made the decision to follow Hangout instead of sticking with Joe. His instinct had told him—

He froze, his hand over his mouth, and felt the blood drain from his face. He closed his eyes and relived that fateful instant when he'd watched Joe and Hangout part company.

His hand began to tremble. He clenched his fist and looked down at his whitened knuckles.

He'd been fooling himself all these months, blocking the truth. He hadn't followed his instinct that night—he'd ignored it in favor of logic. He'd trailed Hangout because it was the logical thing.

Stick with the suspect. That was what he'd been trained to do. Mitch had denied the internal warning that had told him Joe might be in trouble and needing his help.

He reeled from the truth. It had been his *failure* to follow his instinct that had cost Joe his life and Allie her freedom. Not the other way around. He scrubbed at his eyes with his palms as guilt weighed on him like a boulder.

If he made the wrong choice again, Allie would surely die. He had to follow his instinct.

He got on the parkway headed back to D.C.

ALLIE STOOD in the darkened hallway of her former home, once again facing those ominous double doors. This time, however, Mitch wasn't there to comfort her. To keep her calm. Instead, her nerves screamed with apprehension and fear—stone-cold, bone-chilling fear that wrenched the breath from her body and sat like a lead weight in her belly.

Carmine Bongiovi held her future in his hands—her future and her past. He knew what she did not. He knew who had been standing at that door. And now he was waiting impatiently for her to remember the face of the killer.

"Go ahead, Mrs. Barnes. Open the door."

"It's not that simple," she said, her gaze on the brass doorknobs. "Your Taser attack added the association of shock and pain to the opening of the door. That makes it more difficult. I need more time."

"Don't give me that. You ain't one to let anything stand in your way once you've made up your mind to do something. Now close your eyes. Think about what you were doing that night. I've read up on retrograde amnesia. A lot of doctors believe if you put yourself back in the same place, and do the same things you were doing when you lost your memory, it'll come back."

"I've read about that, too. But there's also a good chance I'll never recall those few minutes." She sent Bongiovi an assessing glance. How ruthless was he? "We can't stay here forever, opening and closing doors. What are you going to do if my memory doesn't return?"

"I told you. If you don't get your memory back, you're useless to me." He gave an eloquent shrug.

She remembered Mitch and Fred talking about him, speculating that he was in the pockets of someone in government. "Who are you working for?" she asked, turning to face him.

A movement behind him startled her. She took a step backward.

Two men dressed in dark suits stepped out of the kitchen area at the end of the hall. Semiautomatic pistols gleamed in their hands.

"What the—?" Bongiovi muttered, reaching inside his coat.

"Don't do it, Bongiovi," one of the men said.

"Are you all right, Mrs. Barnes?" The second man's voice was familiar.

Frowning, Allie nodded. Then her mind locked onto his identity. He was Special Agent Sherbourne, Frank Conover's assistant. Allie had met him a few times with Joe. "Yes, I'm fine. What's going on here?"

Another figure stepped out behind the first two. "Hello, Allie."

Allie stared at Deputy Assistant Director Frank Conover. He was impeccably dressed, as always, his designer suit displaying his tall elegance to best advantage. "What are you doing here, Frank?"

"When I heard you'd been kidnapped, I thought the culprit might be Bongiovi. And it seemed obvious that he'd want to finish the job here, where he started it."

"You came yourself? I don't understand."

"Finish the job?" Bongiovi's frantic outburst overrode her words. "Why you—"

"Shut up and put your hands up." The first agent moved toward Bongiovi, who immediately stuck out his hands, palms up.

"Okay. Okay." Sweat beaded on his bald head. "No problem."

Allie barely heard their conversation. She was too busy watching Conover's stoic expression. There was only one reason he would have come himself.

Mitch.

"Frank, why are you here? Is it Mitch?" Her heart squeezed until she thought she would cry from the pain.

"Now, Allie. I wanted to come myself, to make sure you were all right." He slipped his arm around her as if to protect her. She longed to withdraw from his suffocating grasp. He patted her arm. "Try to stay calm."

"Mrs. Barnes," Bongiovi interrupted as the second FBI agent started toward him. "Think about what you just asked me!"

"Shut up," the agent growled.

"Look out!" Conover shouted.

Suddenly, surprisingly, Allie was propelled forward. She stumbled, struggling for balance, and reached out to catch herself. Her feet tangled. She fell toward Bongiovi. His hand grabbed her arm and jerked her upright.

"He's got a gun! Shoot him!"

"Don't move!"

Instinctively, she rammed her elbow backward and balanced on the balls of her feet, but the cold steel of a gun at her neck froze her in place. The gun's muzzle dug into her skin.

"I didn't want it to happen this way." Bongiovi twisted Allie's arm behind her back and held it there. Nauseating pain shot through her shoulder, and tears welled in her eyes. She knew that resisting might tear her rotator cuff or dislocate the joint, so she didn't move.

Instead, she cut her eyes to Conover, who had drawn his weapon and had it trained on Bongiovi.

"He's bluffing," Conover barked. "He won't kill her. Shoot him."

Allie calculated her odds. Bongiovi was shorter than her by approximately three inches, and he had her pressed tightly against him. The agents would have to shoot him in the head to kill him without the bullet going through her first. That thought wasn't promising.

"You may be right, Conover." Bongiovi shifted the barrel of his gun toward Conover. "I'd rather not shoot Mrs. Barnes. Maybe I'll shoot you instead."

"Shoot him!" Conover screamed at his men.

Allie watched the agents from the corner of her eye. They gripped their guns with both hands and with their feet braced apart, ready to fire. But they hesitated.

Allie strained against Bongiovi's strong grip.

"Hold still," he muttered, wrenching her arm a millimeter higher behind her back. Pain knifed her shoulder.

She grimaced and stood still. She didn't want to die.

She wanted to see Mitch again, to thank him for helping her.

Who was she kidding? She wanted to grab him and hold him and never let him go.

One of the agents shifted. He was preparing to fire.

"Mrs. Barnes," Carmine Bongiovi said, backing away with her in tow. "I truly wanted you to remember who killed your husband and shot you in the back. But I'm afraid I'm going to have to take my chances without the benefit of your memory."

Allie recognized the tension in his voice and knew he was about to act. But she didn't have a clue what he might do.

Federal agents were taught to never put a hostage in the line of fire. But Bongiovi held his gun in his right hand, so the agents' only shot was over her right shoulder. Swallowing hard, Allie met Conover's intent gaze. She had to help him. It was the only way she could free herself and survive.

Bongiovi's frenzied voice rang in her ears. "Conover, it's time you—"

She dropped like a rag doll, veering to the left as she fell.

Three shots rang out. She hit the ground hard on her shoulder and rolled, righting herself against the wall, praying no one had been fatally shot in the exchange.

When her vision cleared, the first thing she noticed was the blood. Bongiovi lay on the ground, bright crimson darkening his shoulder. The blood pooled on the blue-veined white tiles like spilled wine. Like the blood that had spilled when Joe was shot.

Conover and the agents—all unhurt—stood over her, their worried faces filling her vision.

"Allie, are you all right?" Conover said briskly.

She nodded, her mouth too dry to speak. She swallowed and licked her lips. "Yes. I'm fine."

Conover shook his head. "That was quick thinking, but it was also a very foolish thing to do." Then he nodded at Sherbourne and the other agent. "You two okay? Then get him out of here." Conover wiped his brow and smoothed his tie.

"Sherbourne, make sure Cates knows how to take care of Mr. Bongiovi. And you keep an eye out. I'll be sure Mrs. Barnes is all right." He exchanged a hard look with Sherbourne. "I need to wrap things up *here.*" His expression darkened. "Remember that meeting I mentioned this morning? Arrange for the participants to be brought here."

Sherbourne glanced at Allie, then nodded.

Conover held out his hand. Allie took it and let him help her to her feet. Her knees were shaky and her shoulder hurt.

"Aren't you going to call the police?" She gulped. "Don't we need to give statements? File reports?"

"Sherbourne will take care of everything. If the police need us, he'll tell them where to find us." Conover patted Allie's hand.

"Mr. Bongiovi said he had information for me." Panic rose up inside her. She'd made her choice, to help Conover, but she still needed the information Bongiovi had. "I need to talk to him."

"Bongiovi is a two-bit crook and a liar." Conover's voice was deep and calm. "Where can we sit down?"

Allie thought a moment. "There's a window seat in Joe's study."

Conover got her seated and sat beside her, her hand

cupped in his. "There. You're shaking. You need some time to catch your breath. That was quite an ordeal."

Allie agreed. But what had started it? How had she fallen? Someone had shoved her.

She leveled her gaze at Conover. "What happened in there? Someone pushed me."

"It all happened so fast. Bongiovi grabbed you and pulled his gun."

"I don't understand. I was at least three feet from him." A dull throbbing echoed through her head, leftover effects from the Taser. "It doesn't seem possible."

"You were upset. You still are."

Allie concentrated, pushing past her headache. "Frank, Bongiovi knows who killed Joe."

Conover's hand stilled. He raised his eyebrows.

"He wouldn't tell me. He wanted me to remember for myself."

A small smile quirked the deputy assistant director's mouth. "Obviously a ploy to make you think he knew something. Well, you don't have to worry about that any more. Obviously, he knows who killed Joe because he did it. Now we have him in custody. Although with those wounds, I wouldn't be surprised if he doesn't make it."

"He couldn't have killed Joe."

Conover glanced narrowly at her. "Why do you say that?"

"Because I'd never met Carmine Bongiovi until today. The man I let into our house that night was someone I knew well."

"You're regaining some of your memory. That's good." He narrowed his eyes. "What else do you remember?"

Allie racked her brain, but she couldn't get past her fear about the reason Conover had sought her out.

Mitch. In all the excitement, she had forgotten. She grabbed Conover's arm. "What about Mitch? You said you wanted to tell me yourself what happened. Where is he? Why didn't he come with you?"

Frank Conover looked her straight in the eye, then blinked and dropped his gaze to his shoes. His shoulders slumped. "I'm sorry, Allie. They did everything they could."

Chapter Thirteen

Mitch turned onto Allie's street and spotted a black sedan with government plates starting a right turn at the next intersection. He only got a glimpse of the vehicle, but it looked like there were two people inside.

He glanced at Allie's house. Should he follow the car? No. Allie could be inside the house. Praying that the instinct he'd never wanted to trust wasn't steering him wrong now, he followed his compulsion to check the house.

He drove down the drive and around to the back where a dark green sedan sat hidden in the garage. The only person he knew with a car like that was Frank Conover, and Conover shouldn't be anywhere near Allie's house. But the government license plate was unmistakable. Mitch's pulse raced.

Was Conover in there with Allie? Mitch should have felt relieved, but his heart pounded harder and his jaw ached with tension. Why had Conover come here? What had happened to his day full of meetings?

Mitch's brain took a leap, past all logical arguments, straight to the most important question looming in his brain. Had Conover murdered Joe?

Immediately, half a dozen reasons why he couldn't have rose up to battle Mitch's conjecture. But what stuck in his head as he killed the car's engine was what Allie had said.

I had to let him in. He was so big. So powerful.

He'd thought at the time that powerful was an odd word to choose. Had Allie's subconscious provided a description, not of the killer's physical appearance, but of what he represented, to her and to Joe?

Deputy assistant director for criminal investigations was a powerful position. It was the position Allie's father had held until his murder.

Mitch punched a button on his cell phone. "Jack. I'm at Allie's house. Get over here. And alert the police. Something's going on."

"What can you tell me?"

"Conover's here. Maybe with Allie. Hurry."

Jack took a deep breath. "Are you saying Conover—"

"I don't know. If I'm wrong, I'll take the heat. But whatever it is, I need backup."

"You got it."

"Come ready for anything. This could be a false alarm. Got to go." Mitch cut the connection and silently opened his car door. He prayed he wasn't too late. Logic told him there was no reason for the killer to keep her alive.

Allie had to be all right. If she weren't, he'd know in his heart, where the flame of his love burned for her. A flame that he knew would flicker and die if she were no longer living. His heart pounding in sudden dread, he eased the car door closed.

"Not so fast."

The voice came from behind Mitch, startling him. He reached for his weapon, and slapped empty leather. Cursing, he whirled, prepared to face the attacker with his bare fists. He'd let himself get distracted with worry over Allie.

Before he could get his weight behind a punch, pain exploded in his head. He stumbled, dazed, a part of his brain aware that he'd been hit by the butt of a gun.

A gun barrel prodded him in the ribs. "Eyes front."

The voice was familiar. "Let's go. Nice of you to drop by. Saved us a lot of time. You've got an appointment to clear up some unfinished business."

"Sherbourne. Deputy Conover's shadow. I should have known you'd be here." Mitch turned, fighting dizziness, and lifted his hands.

The gun left his ribs and immediately pressed into the back of his neck. The metallic chill made him wince. His first instinct was to flip Sherbourne and disarm him. He was almost certain he could do it, but he knew that wasn't the wisest choice. He needed to get inside the house without alerting Conover.

"Where's Allie?" he asked.

"You haven't figured that out yet? She's the unfinished business."

"No!" ALLIE CRIED. "He can't be dead." She couldn't accept what Frank Conover had told her. "I'd know." She stood and paced, the anguish in her heart belying her brave words. The place inside her that ached with longing, that pulsed with love, would be empty if he were gone. "Take me to see him."

"Now, Allie," Conover said, rising and reaching for her. "I know this is a lot to take in, but try to remember he was only trying to protect you."

Allie pulled away. She didn't want comfort. She wanted proof. She would never believe he was dead until she saw him with her own eyes.

"Frank, please, take me to Mitch," she said tightly, clenching her fists, holding on to her last shred of control with every ounce of strength she had left.

Conover watched her closely as he reached into his coat pocket and pulled out a tin of breath mints. He offered them to her. She shook her head. She didn't want a damn mint. He was wasting time. Her nails bit into her palms as she resisted the impulse to slap the things out of his hand.

Conover opened the tin and took out a mint, then clicked the container closed and slid it back into his pocket. He popped the mint into his mouth. "We'll leave in a few minutes. I'm waiting for something."

"What? A phone call? Don't you have a cell phone?" She could hear the edge of hysteria in her voice.

Conover put his hand on the small of her back and bent his head close to hers. "Why don't you sit down? It'll all be over soon. You've had a rough few days. I'm sure you're exhausted."

The smell of wintergreen mint on his breath nearly knocked her down. Her head spun and her thoughts whirled crazily as memories sliced through her like a cutting winter wind.

She was back there, at the door, looking at the man wrapped totally in black. The sharp odor of mint burned her nostrils as icy air swirled around him. Scattered flakes of snow turned to drops of water on the man's black wool overcoat as he lifted his head out of the concealing wool scarf.

"Allie?"

The smell. The chill. The sound of his voice.

She gasped. She was standing in the presence of Joe's murderer.

She recoiled, backing up until her legs hit the window seat. "Oh, dear God."

Conover's expression changed to a benevolent smile. "So you've finally remembered." His movements methodical, he unbuttoned his jacket and pulled out his gun. "Now please, sit down."

Allie tried to sort out the confusing information bombarding her, but it was like fighting through a thick fog. "Wh-why?" It was the best she could manage.

Conover's gun didn't waver a millimeter as he picked a speck of lint from his sleeve. "Why should you sit down? Because I told you to." His voice was cold.

Fingers of dread danced up her spine.

Conover continued. "Why did I kill Joe? Because that idiot Bongiovi wouldn't do it. Anything but murder, he told me. He didn't like killing. He'd only committed murder with his own hands once in his life. When he shot your father to ensure his rise to power."

The whole truth settled over her like a suffocating blanket. She squeezed her eyes shut. Standing in front of her were all her nightmares embodied in one evil man.

"It was you. You had my father killed." Her voice sounded small, even to her. That was the information Bongiovi had hoped to bargain with.

Conover shrugged. "It was a quid pro quo. Bongiovi took care of getting your father out of the way so I could advance in the Bureau, and I ensured his position as the city's major crime lord. It's the law of reciprocity."

"But why kill Joe?"

A tight smile arced his lips. "Your husband was threatening me. He just wouldn't stop working on your father's murder. Bongiovi offered to send someone else to do it, but I couldn't take a chance with a small-time hit man. I had to be absolutely sure Joe couldn't tell what he'd discovered. Joe had potential. I thought he'd understood the compromises. But it turned out he was working to get Bongiovi a plea agreement for testifying against me. *Me.* I had to do something. Without Joe in the picture, I still had a hold over Bongiovi. So I had to do it myself. There was no one else I could trust."

Allie's memories were crystal clear—horrifyingly clear—thanks to the odor of wintergreen. Conover had spoken to her, seeming surprised to see her, and then walked past her, right up to Joe and shot him between the eyes. "You were his boss, his mentor. Your wife and I were friends." Her stomach churned with nausea.

"You were a complication I didn't expect. Every Wednesday evening, you met with the Bureau's Community Outreach Program. *Every Wednesday.* Why were you home that night?"

Allie didn't bother answering his question. Instead, she swallowed against the revulsion she felt and sat up straight. She lifted her chin and looked him in the eye. "You can't possibly believe you can get away with this."

"I've gotten away with it so far. And right now everything is going according to plan."

Allie studied the deputy assistant director, looking for any weak point, a way to possibly overpower him. "So what is your plan? I'm certain it involves shooting me. You'd just better be sure you do it right this time.

Because if you fail, I will make sure you pay—for my father, for my husband, for Mitch."

Mitch. Pain doubled her over. She wrapped her arms around herself, whether to hold herself together or to try to keep the pain at bay, she didn't know. How could she live without him?

Conover gestured impatiently with his free hand. "I can't just shoot you in cold blood, as much as I'd like to. That would be too hard to explain. When you escaped the explosion in your apartment and ran to Decker, I had to come up with an alternate plan. It took me a while, but I have to admit it's a good one." He glanced at his watch. "My assistant should be calling soon, to let me know that they've located Decker, and are on their way here."

Allie's heart lurched. "Located Mitch? He's not—"

"Of course not. It was just a liquid Taser blast, just like you got. They rarely do any permanent damage." He shook his head, laughing softly. "It *was* entertaining to see how much the idea of his death affected you."

Relief drained the strength from Allie's limbs. "Oh, God, thank you," she whispered.

"Don't thank me yet." His mouth twitched. "Your propensity for weak men will make it easy to set up your deaths as a murder/suicide and eliminate a number of problems at once."

"Weak? You bastard." A jolt of fury fed strength to Allie's body. "You're the one who committed murder to get where you are, and you dare to call decent, honorable men weak? You must be out of your mind."

Caught up in his plan, he paid no attention to her outburst. "Grant Irby offered me an unexpected stroke of luck when he planted that evidence in Decker's apartment and then arranged for an anonymous tip. When the police searched Decker's place, they discovered a pair of his shoes with your blood on the soles. The shoe print matched an incorrectly tagged photo in the evidence box. They also found a receipt for a rental car for the night of Joe's death. A black Town Car, paid for in cash. There may have been one or two other items." He waved a hand. "I don't remember."

Allie listened in horrified disbelief. "That's absurd. You're going to try to prove that *Mitch* killed Joe and tried to kill me?"

"On its face, the planted evidence is weak, but combined with the fact that Decker shot you and then himself right here at your house once you remembered that he was Joe's killer—"

"No one will believe Mitch would murder Joe."

He laughed. "Of course they will. People love a good scandal. And Irby did an excellent job of planting the possibility during your deposition and Decker's that you two were having an affair." Conover paused and looked at her expectantly. "I've always wondered. Were you?"

Allie sent him a look of disgust. "Go to hell."

Conover shrugged. "So, to continue the scenario, when Joe found out about the affair, you ended it. But Mitch wouldn't accept that. He killed Joe. You tried to stop him, threatening to go to the police, so he had to shoot you. Something interrupted him and he didn't finish—" Conover halted and cocked his head, listening.

Allie heard footsteps on the marble floor of the hall.

"Ah. Here's the rest of my plan now. It's about time you got here."

Mitch appeared in the doorway, a trickle of blood drying on the side of his face and his hands raised in surrender. Behind him, Sherbourne held a handgun, its deadly barrel pointed at the nape of Mitch's neck. The sight sent terror racing through Allie's blood. But the terror couldn't block out her thrill of relief at seeing him alive. She jumped up, swaying with reaction, and caught herself against the wall. "Mitch! Thank God!"

He met her gaze for a fraction of a second, but Allie read his message as if he'd shouted it. *Hang in there.* She read something else, too. His blue eyes were filled with relief and that beautiful tenderness that he reserved for her.

"Good job, Sherbourne." Conover looked pleased. "Get him in here."

Mitch took a step forward. Allie almost cried out when Sherbourne pushed the barrel of the gun farther into Mitch's neck with hands that shook. Sherbourne's prominent Adam's apple jerked as he swallowed. His eyes were wide, panicked. He was nervous about something, and nervous people with guns were doubly dangerous. Allie couldn't take her eyes off the gun barrel.

"Deputy Conover, what's going on here?" Mitch asked, his brow furrowing in puzzlement. "Sherbourne's got a gun on me and you've got one on Allie?"

"Shut up, Decker. I've had enough of you." Conover glowered at Mitch. "Now, do you want to shoot Allie yourself, or would you rather watch me do it?"

Rather than the shock Allie expected, Mitch's lips curved in an innocent smile. "How about a third choice?"

Conover laughed shortly. "Don't screw with me, Decker. I don't have the time."

"I'm perfectly serious. I was thinking that I'd take you into custody."

"Custody? You really are an arrogant—"

Conover stopped talking as Sherbourne lowered his gun. Behind Mitch, Jack O'Hara and Ray Storm stepped into the doorway, their weapons trained on Conover. He turned pale.

"Allie, move away from him," Mitch snapped.

Allie did as she was told.

"Conover, put down your weapon."

Behind Mitch, Sherbourne started blubbering. "I'm sorry, boss. They got the drop on me. Then they offered me a deal. I've got a family—"

"Shut up." Conover's voice sounded frantic. He looked down at his gun and then up at Mitch. An odd smile quirked his lips. "It looks like *I* have three choices now."

"Put it down, Frank. It's over." Mitch took a step toward him. "We picked up Cates a little while ago. Carmine Bongiovi was bleeding all over his car, but oddly enough, Cates wasn't headed toward a hospital. No need to worry, though. The police got Bongiovi to the emergency room. It looks like he'll live to testify about who killed Joe." Mitch glanced at Allie, his gaze sending her reassurance.

"Like I said, I have three choices now." Conover's hard gaze flickered to Allie. "I can kill her before your guys can get off a shot. I can shoot you." He pointed the gun at Mitch.

Allie's heart beat in triple time. Mitch didn't have a gun.

But then Conover shrugged and sighed. "Or I can—"

Allie watched in stunned disbelief as Frank Conover turned the gun on himself and squeezed the trigger.

At the same instant, Mitch dove forward. Time moved like a video in slow motion.

"No!" Mitch shouted as he stretched out his arms to deflect Conover's shot. Their bodies collided just as the gun fired and for an endless instant the two men froze, locked together in midair.

Then, with a grunt, they fell. O'Hara and Storm were already on them before they hit the ground. Storm reached for Conover, and O'Hara grabbed Mitch. Mitch's hands were still wrapped around Conover's. He'd almost succeeded in deflecting the man's shot.

The two agents pulled the men apart. Storm dragged Conover's limp body into the middle of the floor, leaving a trail of blood that leaked from Conover's head.

"It's just a graze," Storm said. "He'll probably walk out of here." Storm pulled handcuffs from his belt and jerked Conover's hands behind his back.

"Decker's clean as a whistle." O'Hara helped Mitch upright, then let go to see if he could stand alone. "Well, almost." He gestured to the blood caking the side of Mitch's face. Then he turned his attention to Sherbourne, who was cowering in the corner, and took his gun.

"How'd you like playing with an empty gun for a change?" Jack said as he collared him. Then he lifted his head, listening. He grinned. "I do believe I hear the police, right on time."

Allie hadn't breathed since O'Hara and Storm had stepped into the doorway. She took a long, shaky breath and walked over to Mitch, who was staring down at Conover's gun.

O'Hara held out an evidence bag he'd fished out of his pocket. Mitch dropped the gun into it.

Allie touched the side of his head, where flecks of dried blood clung to his skin. "They hurt you," she whispered.

"Just a conk on the head." He smiled at her with his mouth, but his eyes stayed grave. "A small price to pay to find you safe."

"Frank told me you were dead." Remembering the pain that had lanced through her then, she wobbled.

Concern and anger darkened his gaze as he caught her arm to steady her. "Hey, it's okay. It's all over now." He touched her cheek.

"I didn't believe him." She couldn't drag her gaze from his face. "If you'd been killed, I'd have known."

He searched her gaze and was about to speak. But he pressed his lips together instead as the sirens got louder and police swarmed into the house.

It was over two hours before they were finally able to leave. Mitch watched Allie carefully as worry etched fresh scars on his heart. She was growing paler by the minute, and as grueling as the officers' repetitive questions were for him, he knew they must be twice as bad for her.

Finally, he spoke to the senior detective on the scene and then walked over to the window seat where Allie waited, her hands clasped together in her lap. He sat down next to her and put his hand over hers.

She looked up, her green eyes dull with exhaustion.

"The chief of detectives just gave me some information. Bongiovi is awake. He's offering information on your father's murder plus more against Conover in exchange for immunity." Mitch nodded toward the other side of the room where Sherbourne was nodding eagerly at a police officer. "Also, Sherbourne will cooperate."

Allie looked back at her hands. "What about the charges against you? Are they going to do anything to that piece of scum Irby?"

"Oh, yeah. He'll probably be charged with tampering with evidence, fraud and conspiracy to cover up a murder. He's liable to spend quite a lot of time in prison. He'll enjoy that."

She nodded but didn't smile.

"Come on," he said, squeezing her hand. "Let's get out of here."

Hope and gratitude shone in her eyes. "Really? We can go?" She stood and swayed.

Mitch reached out to steady her.

"Sorry. I'm just so tired."

"You have a right to be. We have permission to finish up our statements in the morning. Jack's going to drive us. I'll be glad to take you—" He stopped when her gaze met his, sad and frightened and a little lost. He knew what she was thinking. She didn't have anywhere to go.

"We'll go to my apartment. It'll probably be a mess because of the search, but you're welcome to stay there until you decide what you're going to do."

"Thank you," she said tightly, walking past him and out of her dead husband's study, leaving Mitch to wonder at the tinge of irony in her voice.

Chapter Fourteen

Mitch was right. The apartment was a mess. The CSI team had gone through everything, and left it all right where they'd finished with it.

He picked up a pile of clothes off his bed and tossed them into his closet, and straightened the mattress. He'd deal with the rest of the clutter later. Right now, his priority was taking care of Allie.

He rooted around in the clothes they'd dumped out of his dresser and came up with a Golden Gate Bridge T-shirt his sister's kids had given him last Christmas.

Allie showered first and stayed under the running water until he began to worry about her. Finally, she emerged wearing his T-shirt, her dark red hair falling in damp curls around her face and her eyes bloodshot and puffy. He realized that, like their first night together, she'd been crying in the shower.

He couldn't blame her. The intense trauma and shock she'd been through today was more than anyone should have to endure in a lifetime. And still, even though she'd been Tasered, kidnapped—not once but twice—and nearly killed, she still hadn't complained.

She had cried alone in the shower instead.

"Hey," he said, smiling at her. "Want some coffee? I've got plenty of sugar."

Even with red, puffy eyes and wet hair, she was beautiful. He could spend the rest of his life just watching her as she showered, as she ate, as she lay beneath him, her lips moist and her eyes dewy bright—

"No."

Mitch wrenched his thoughts back. He must be more tired than he'd realized.

"Thank you, but I think I just need to—" She gestured toward the bed, her eyes filling with tears. "It's been a long day."

"I know it has. Just give me a few minutes to shower and I'll be out of your way."

Their gazes met and locked, and Mitch saw that Allie had no more idea of how to act with him than he did with her, now that danger no longer surrounded them. He wanted to hold her and promise her that all the bad in her life was gone. He wanted to lie beside her in his bed with her body molded against his, and tell her that he had always loved her and he always would.

But what he wanted wasn't important.

He'd made a vow to Joe and to himself to take care of her, and he would keep that vow. She had a lot to deal with. She didn't need him adding complications.

He cleared his throat. "So, I'll just go shower."

Allie nodded.

Twenty minutes later, when Mitch emerged from the bathroom, wearing cotton pajama pants, the lights were out and Allie was asleep. He stood at the foot of the bed for a few seconds, watching her sleep and listening to her soft, even breathing. He felt like a Peeping Tom, but he couldn't help himself. She was so beautiful, so fragile and yet so strong. Her creamy skin glowed in the pale light from the streetlamps overlooking the park, and her damp red curls fanned out over his pillow, making his fingers itch to touch them. But he couldn't do it.

His body tight with unslaked desire, he turned away and went into the living room and collapsed on the couch, tucking one arm behind his head.

As tired as he was, the sight of Allie in his bed had stirred him. Irritated at his lack of self-control, he closed his eyes and tried to relax. His muscles still twitched occasionally from the aftereffects of the Taser. Behind his closed eyelids, the events of the past four days raced across his inner vision like a slide show gone out of control. He shifted restlessly. There was no way he could sleep.

With a sigh, he got up and poured himself a cup of coffee then stepped out onto his balcony. The moon was half-full and added its pale glow to the streetlamps. Sitting in a framed porch swing, he drank his coffee and tried to shake off the pall of loss and loneliness that was settling over him.

Things were falling into place for Allie. She'd finally be able to put the heartache of the past behind her, to lay her father's and husband's ghosts to rest and move on with her life.

He should be happy for her. He was. He arched his stiff neck. Tomorrow would be a grueling day, with all the interviews, statements and endless questions. He tried to catalog the events of the past days in his head, but he couldn't concentrate.

His thoughts kept returning to Allie, asleep in his bed. To him, it seemed so right for her to be there. He shook his head.

She wouldn't think so. The only reason she'd agreed to come with him was because she didn't have anywhere else to go.

She'd asked him for one thing and one thing only. Help her find Joe's killer so she could put the FBI and everyone connected with it behind her.

Mitch squeezed his coffee mug between his palms, a new thought arising in his mind. What if, by some miracle, she couldn't live without him? He shook his head wryly at his fanciful thoughts.

Still, what if she asked him to walk away? Could he? Washington, D.C., was his home. The Bureau was his family, especially the Division of Unsolved Mysteries. Each member of his team held a special place in his heart.

Could he give all that up for her? He ran his hand through his short hair and down to the tense muscles at the back of his neck.

Yes. He could. If he had to.

But she wouldn't ask.

She'd already made her feelings clear. When she looked at him, she saw the personification of everything she'd lost, everything the Bureau had taken from her. His face was the face of the FBI.

Despite his whirling thoughts, Mitch's weariness caught up with him and he found himself nodding off to sleep. He set down his mug and propped his feet on the balcony rail. His eyes drifted shut. His body finally relaxed.

"Mitch?"

He came awake instantly, on guard, unsure of how long he'd slept. Then he remembered. The danger was over. He was on his balcony. He sat up. Allie was standing in front of him, the moon glowing on her face like heavenly light illuminating an angel.

"Hey, Allie. Did something wake you?" His T-shirt came just below mid-thigh on her, and her bare legs were sleek and golden in the pale light. Her hair was a mass of waves and curls, and her eyes looked big and frightened.

"I woke up alone, and for a minute I couldn't remember where I was. Why didn't you come to bed?"

Because I can't just lie there next to you. He shook his head without comment. "Want to sit down?"

She perched beside him like a skittish bird. For a few minutes, they just sat together, swinging gently, not speaking.

"Joe knew Frank Conover had my father killed."

Mitch looked at her. Her hands were in her lap, her head was bent and her shoulders were hunched. She raised her head and met his gaze, tears glittering in her eyes.

He took her hand and pulled it to rest on his knee, caressing her knuckles with his thumb.

"That's why he was dealing with Bongiovi." She wiped away a tear. "He was trying to get proof."

"That's what it looks like." Mitch didn't know what else to say. He wasn't sure if she needed reassurance, or if she just needed to talk. "You were right all along. Joe wasn't doing anything underhanded."

Allie nodded and peered down at Mitch's large elegant hand cradling hers. The gentle friction of his thumb stroking her knuckles was both soothing and erotic.

"I didn't like waking up and not knowing where you were. I couldn't find you."

"I'm sorry, I should have—"

"Mitch." She stopped him. "I saw you sitting out

here and it felt like I'd found something I'd been searching for forever."

His thumb stilled and his body grew tense. Caution radiated from him like heat from a furnace.

"You're exhausted, Allie." Mitch's throat moved as he swallowed. "You're distraught. So much has happened in such a short time."

"Yes. A lot has happened." She pulled her hand away and turned toward him. Her heart pounded so loud she was sure he could hear it. Her hands trembled, and her breathing grew fast and shallow. She was scared of what the next few minutes might hold.

She knew the kind of man Mitch was. He would never break a sacred trust. He'd promised Joe he would take care of her, and that's what he'd done—was still doing. There was a good chance he'd never get past the fact that she had been Joe's wife.

But she'd looked deep into his eyes. She'd made love with him. If she was wrong, she'd walk away. She couldn't be, though. Not about this.

"Look at me, Mitch."

His throat jerked and he turned his head. His gaze was guarded, his jaw set.

Allie touched his cheek and felt the muscles working under his skin. "You've loved me for a long time, haven't you?"

Mitch blanched, and he rose abruptly, stalking over to the balcony rail. Rain had begun to fall, turning the streetlights into hazy bubbles and the night sky into a soft gray blanket.

Allie got up and stood beside him. His hands gripped the wood railing, his knuckles bone-white and beginning to bead with rain.

"Joe was my boss and my friend," he said tightly. "He trusted me to take care of you."

She put her hand on his bare arm. His skin was hot. Hot and wet and enticing. "I know. And I know you would have died to protect me. You're the most honorable man I've ever known. But honor isn't everything."

Turning his head, Mitch's haunted blue eyes met hers. "Sometimes it's the only thing."

She nodded. He'd built his life—his career—on honor. If she knew him, and she was sure she did, then honor was what was holding him back now. With apprehension clogging her throat, Allie took a deep breath. "I love you."

A pained expression crossed his face, and a fissure opened up in Allie's heart. She'd done everything she could. She'd given him all she had. It was up to him now. He had to step out from behind his shield of honor and open up to her.

"You hate the Bureau. Look what it's done to you."

"Look what it's given me."

His eyes glistened in the hazy light. There were droplets of water on his cheeks and shoulders and abdomen. Allie felt the rain peppering the heated skin of her face.

Mitch ducked his head. "You're right. I've loved you from the first moment I ever saw you." His voice was rough with emotion. He looked up, his expression bleak. "But that didn't matter. What mattered then was that you trusted me. What matters now is that you're free and safe, and you can put the past and the Bureau behind you, like you've wanted to do."

"You know," she said, looking out over the park, "I believe that we each glean something from everyone we have ever known. I learned from Joe that friendship can be as important as love." Her eyes stung and her voice faltered. "I miss Joe. I'll always miss him." But the love she had shared with Joe had not been the greatest love of her life.

"I miss him, too." Mitch's voice was unsteady.

Allie swallowed and blinked as a raindrop caught on her eyelashes. "I learned from you that love can grow from friendship. And I learned that there was a lot I didn't know about love, until I made love with you."

She peered up at his harshly handsome face, shiny with raindrops. "I know who you are, Mitch Decker. And I know that your job does not define you. It's your honor and integrity and your infinite capacity for selfless caring that makes you the man I will love until I die."

Mitch grimaced and closed his eyes, and her heart shattered. He couldn't do it. He couldn't get past what he considered his betrayal of Joe's trust.

Disappointment drained the last of her strength. Allie realized she'd been holding herself up by sheer force of will. "I guess I should try to get some sleep," she said in a small voice. "Tomorrow's going to be a long day."

She started to go and then stopped. She put her palm on Mitch's cheek. His eyes opened.

"Thank you, Mitch," she said, as tears spilled over from her eyes to mingle with the rain. "Thank you for saving me. And thank you for loving me."

Before she could lower her hand, he caught her wrist and slid her palm across his lips, kissing it gently.

Hope flickered in the deepest recesses of her broken heart.

"Do you think we'd sleep better in the same bed?" he murmured against her palm.

Not daring to anticipate what he meant, she nodded carefully. "I know I would."

He lowered her hand and held it in both of his. "That's the problem. I'm pretty sure I wouldn't."

Allie swallowed. "You wouldn't?"

Mitch's gaze softened and his lips turned up in a gentle smile. "In the past few days, I've discovered that sleeping beside you is next to impossible. But it *is* my second favorite thing in the world to do."

Laughter bubbled up from Allie's chest as her heart stopped aching and began to flutter with happiness. "Just your second favorite? Then what's your most favorite thing?"

Mitch pulled her close. She shivered at the cool drops of water on her hot skin. The thin layers of cotton between them did nothing to hide the proof of his desire. Feeling him hard and pulsing against her belly made her thighs and her insides tremble.

He lifted her chin and kissed her tenderly. "Want me to show you?" he whispered in her ear.

And before she could even form an answer, he lifted her in his arms and carried her through the balcony doors to his bed.

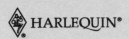

HARLEQUIN®

INTRIGUE®

presents brand-new installments of

HEROES, INC.

from *USA TODAY* bestselling author
Susan Kearney

HIJACKED
HONEYMOON
(HI #808, November 2004)

PROTECTOR S.O.S.
(HI #814, December 2004)

Available at your favorite retail outlet.

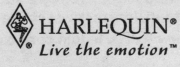

HARLEQUIN®
Live the emotion™

www.eHarlequin.com

If you enjoyed what you just read,
then we've got an offer you can't resist!

Take 2 bestselling love stories FREE!

Plus get a FREE surprise gift!

**Bestselling fantasy author Mercedes Lackey
turns traditional fairy tales on their heads
in the land of the Five Hundred Kingdoms.**

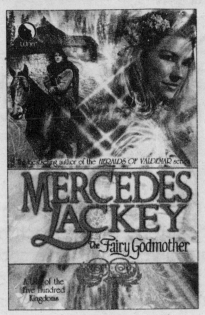

Elena, a Cinderella in the making, gets an
unexpected chance to be a Fairy Godmother. But being a
Fairy Godmother is hard work and she gets into trouble by
changing a prince who is destined to save the kingdom,
into a donkey—but he really deserved it!

Can she get things right and save the kingdom?
Or will her stubborn desire to teach this ass
of a prince a lesson get in the way?

*On sale November 2004.
Visit your local bookseller.*

Like a phantom in the night
comes an exciting promotion from

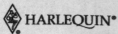
HARLEQUIN®

GOTHIC ROMANCE

Look for a provocative
gothic-themed thriller each month
by your favorite Intrigue authors!
Once you surrender to the classic
blend of chilling suspense and
electrifying romance in these
gripping page-turners, there will
be no turning back....

Available wherever Harlequin books are sold.

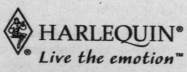

HARLEQUIN®
Live the emotion™

www.eHarlequin.com

HIE3